Awakening of the Divine

Alaric Cross

Copyright © 2024 by Alaric Cross

All rights reserved.

No portion of this book may be reproduced in any form without written permission from the publisher or author, except as permitted by U.S. copyright law.

Contents

1. Chapter 1 — 1
2. Chapter 2 — 4
3. Chapter 3 — 10
4. Chapter 4 — 14
5. Chapter 5 — 19
6. Chapter 6 — 25
7. Chapter 7 — 28
8. Chapter 8 — 34
9. Chapter 9 — 40
10. Chapter 10 — 45
11. Chapter 11 — 51
12. Chapter 12 — 58
13. Chapter 13 — 63
14. Chapter 14 — 68
15. Chapter 15 — 74
16. Chapter 16 — 79
17. Chapter 17 — 84

18.	Chapter 18	89
19.	Chapter 19	94
20.	Chapter 20	119
21.	Chapter 21	128
22.	Chapter 22	133
23.	Chapter 23	138
24.	Chapter 24	143
25.	Chapter 25	150
26.	Chapter 26	155
27.	Chapter 27	160
28.	Chapter 28	165
29.	Chapter 29	170
30.	Chapter 30	177
31.	Chapter 31	183
32.	Chapter 32	189
33.	Chapter 33	196
34.	Chapter 34	204
35.	Chapter 35	210
36.	Chapter 36	217
37.	Chapter 37	222
38.	Chapter 38	229
39.	Chapter 39	235
40.	Chapter 40	240

41.	Chapter 41	244
42.	Chapter 42	254
43.	Epilogue	261

Chapter 1

2023

Mr. Richardson, a scientist who loves his job, has found out about a way to manipulate the human gene. He talks with his wife, Charity, about his discovery. Both Mr. and Mrs. Richardson are scientific geniuses who specialize in human biology and genetics-the best every history book will ever talk about.

A few weeks after their discovery, a governor visits and assigns them to mutate soldiers. He talks to the sweet couple with pride in a manipulative tone. *Well, well, I heard that my favorite scientists have finally found out how to manipulate the human gene-just as I always trusted you would do.*

Mr. Richardson, surprised and confused, asks the proud governor, *Why do you think... I mean, how did you find out what we achieved? We know no one in this city, and I haven't even written an article about my discovery yet.Mr. Governor, could it be that the government is spying on our private lives? We trusted that everyone offline had privacy they could live with. Or is this one of the many lies you make people believe? Hmm, who the hell could be close enough to us to be able to find exactly this information? It's stressing me out! At least give me answers, Mr. Governor!*

The governor is mad. *Who the hell do you think you are to be giving me commands like that?!* he shouts and adds, *Even if I were willing to give you any information, now that you have shown me how disrespectful you can be, I wouldn't anymore, Mark!So listen, without arguing too much, this is an order and a mission you have to fulfill!We have assigned potential soldiers to sacrifice their lives and make this work. You are going to use them all, and then, after finishing your magic trick, give us your formula. I will check in on you once every year, and don't even think about messing with me, or else everyone you have known dies with you! Have a wonderful life!* The governor leaves with a wide smile on his face.

Later, at the governor's office

The governor is thinking about what happened at the Richardsons. His real mission from the government is to get the Richardsons to mutate soldiers for one simple reason. To rule over every country and create one government for the entire world. The idea is to eliminate the "split" governments of the other countries and become godlike.The governor realizes a letter of apology is needed to seal their plan. He thinks of an excuse to apologize for his rudeness.

The letter explains a secret plan for helping mankind evolve. The U.S. government has decided to start with continent H and work its way through the others. The biggest plan is to mutate human beings to an extent, to live longer, and to conquer various planets and make them habitable.

Human beings should be strong enough to face any threat without dying out. This will be a game changer, an invention or discovery that will surpass every generation to ever exist.

Of course, almost everything the letter says is a lie. The government will do anything, even kill and lie to people, just to achieve its dirty, nasty goals. The mission is named Mission Zed, meta-mutated superhuman. „Gene Z".

At the Richardsons

Mr. Richardson, after reading the governor's letter, asks his wife, *Charity, love, what do you think about the government's idea? Do they have the best intentions to help mankind evolve?I have this bad feeling about it.What does your intuition tell you?I think it's finally time to have the son we were planning on having. He should be the first Gene Z and make things better.I put my trust in him. He might be one of the chosen, as this thing in my dream had written on it.I have an idea. How about we ask Jacob and Marine to have this child as their own and raise him, just in case things run out of hand and everything starts getting bad?What do you think, Charr?*

Charity is impressed by her husband's master plan and asks him how he knows their child will be a boy. Her husband answers, *Just a feeling, love, just a feeling.*

They visit and talk with Jacob and Marine, a couple unable to bear fruit, to see if they are ready and willing to have their baby after his birth and being gifted with the Gene Z.

Jacob, without hesitation, accepts the offer with all terms and conditions to make the child theirs and love him for the rest of their lives.

Chapter 2

Three years later - 2026

After experimenting and sacrificing innocent soldiers' life, the Richardsons have finally figured out a way to make it work.

They also find out the process is more effective when used on a child in growth, perfect for their plot to betray the government. During Charity's pregnancy, she hides herself from the rest of the world, except from her family and Jacob.

In the year 2027, She gives birth to a beautiful baby boy and names him John, she overules her husband's Manny. They forge a birth certificate and other important documents, stating that John Freeze is the biological son of Jacob and Marine Freeze.

Charity and her husband begin the experiments on John, right after he takes his first steps. The experiment is done secretly and is ended after six years on John's seventh birthday.

The experiment is over and successful. John is still alive and well. A few months later, they notice how their kid has changed and see something unique in him. They say their last goodbye to their son, who will now have no ties bound to them. They hand him over to his new parents and get back to working with the soldiers.

2040

Six years have passed by. John is thirteen and has decided to visit his biological parents. He wants to show them something amazing, but...

Before John left the Richardsons he vistited Jacob and Marine often, he already knew they were going to be his parents.

John lives happy life with Jacob and Marine. They love him, one could say, more than they promised they would do. They always give him everything he needs, what they can offer. They help him understand his abilities. Underneath their house is a massive hall in which he can move and destroy as much as needed. His real power lies in nature.

They call him a magician.

He taps into the energy surrounding him. Moving a chair without the need to touch is an easy task for him.

Telekinesis, nice one!

Currently, he only has control from a specific area with a specific amount of mass. John isn't yet strong enough to handle everything by himself. Marine is always surprised every time he uses his abilities to finish up tasks.

She thinks it's cute.

Even as a young teenager, John's strength surpasses many grown-ups. Marine, though she thinks John is too young, too cute and innocent, doesn't ever hide his nature and history from him. *He needs to know everything to build up his personality. John is a smart boy and will become a good man one day!*, she always tells her husband.

John believes he is the only gifted human being in the world. He has never met anyone like him. He dreams of becoming someone who will make sure his rules are everyone's rules - absolute!! To bring balance, piece, harmony. He believes it is the only way he can help the world. Until then he, will hold back and try not to hurt anyone.

Violence leads to destruction and doesn't help anyone achieve his goal, not always, he tells himself, with a comforted voice.

He pledges, *Even though I'm this powerful – probably the most powerful to ever exist, I won't turn evil, nor will I have the thought of destroying someone because of something he did, might do, or could do. I am the personification of happiness, love and peace – I will be the hero to save us all!*

What a man! He has a high purpose and an amazing goal in this life. Will he be able to fulfil this promise? Is his goal too much to take on one's self? It might be too much of a burden. What do you think?

His training is working well and school is fun, he states. He loves playing the hero in every situation he and his friends get into. He discovers different perspectives of his powers. He has just learned to sense kinds of auras and knows to whom or what an aura belongs to, the main flow of life.

On a Friday...

John is walking home alone as he usually does, but today he has decided to take a new route. Instead of walking through the big city, he uses to walk through, he walks around it, through a smaller one. *It's much longer, should be fun*, he whispers to himself.

A few minutes in...

He meets an old man meditating in his garden. He looks peaceful. John greets the him and asks if it is ok to join him on his peaceful trip.

The old man doesn't deny his request and answers, *of course kid, you sure can join me. You know, meditating helps the human body rest and build up a strong soul. I could try explaining to you why meditating is good, and what good it does to a human being but I am afraid you do not have enough time today, do you? First, you have to work out and become stronger, only then will meditating have the best effect on you. Though, I do have the feeling we will be meeting up quite often. What you want to call me is up to you. Give me a name that suits your tongue. What is your name young boy?*

John answers, *I'm John but my friends call me Johnny or just J, and as for you, I will call you Grandpa, you are nice and old and wise. I hope, maybe you will help me with more than just meditating. Are you good in the subject they call physics? You know, I have this big secret thing going on and it can change history. Maybe for now, let's be friends and learn a little about each other. You can be my first old friend, what do you think?*

Grandpa accepts the friendship and teaches him how to concentrate and meditate. This goes on for an hour.

He goes home after his peaceful hours and tells his mother about his day and the new old friend he has made. After a short nap, he decides to visit his biological parents throughout the weekend and picks up clothes for a weekend.

The next day

John arrives at his hometown. He recognizes the sweet smell of nature filled with something unfamilliarly different. It smells unpleasant.

Is this iron? No, iron smells different. I'm not only smelling - more smelling and sensing. I sense an aura being exposed, much more than usually. I sense danger.I sense life and something else, is this death? It is death! I've never sensed death before, why would I think it is death? The dead soldiers from our basement... What is this? Why am I having this weird feeling in my stomach? Wait, I don't sense my parents. I can't hear their voices. Are they out on vacation? No, they should be too busy to go on vacation. Wait, I sense them, they are the exposed auras, mixed with others. Are they like me? How are they able to expose their aura this much? This is scary! I have to find out what is happening! Come on move faster boy!

These thoughts run through his head for three minutes straight.

He tries moving faster, but it seems something is scaring him off. He slaps himself several times until he is finally able to move faster. The moment he arrives at his house, he discovers something more unpleasant than what he was sensing. Freshly killed corps, dead bodies laying around, starting from their hall. All of them with wide opened eyes.

He walks over them until he reaches his parent's laboratory. There, he finds his parents, dead.

Everything, every single voice around him cancels out. He is frozen for a minute, then bursts out in rage.

Every tinniest particle, visible and invisible to the eye gets blown away. Every object made out of glass bursts, and the frequency of sound is unbearable to the human ear, like a nuclear explosion.

John unlocks a different side of his. His eyes glow red!

Chapter 3

John has just arrived at his parent's house. Seeing them on their laboratory floor makes him burst out of rage, and his eyes glow red. Everything made out of glass shatters under pressure.

40 minutes before John's arrival

The governor is at Richardson's, a few years after his last visit, and asks about the project.

Charity tells him that 16 years aren't enough to figure out an effective way to generate the new gene and asks him why he hasn't waited for a year before checking up on them.

The governor is angry. He asks about the project three more times, ignoring every word Charity says. She informs her husband about the issue with the governor. Mr. Richardson, knowing what they have done, gets a bad feeling about the whole situation and walks upstairs to talk to the governor before losing her temper.

Mr. Governer, just as my wife has tried explaining the situation to you, it is very hard to generate this gene within a human cell. We have already lost hundreds of soldiers' lives. What else do you want us to do?We can't just risk so many lives.We need to be sure every single mistake made in the previous experiment is solved before we move on to the next patient.

The governor becomes angrier and shouts, *DO YOU THINK I'M THAT STUPID? WHAT DO YOU TAKE ME FOR?*

After shouting, he calms down and continues with a calm but arrogant tone: *Ok folks, I get it. I get you are really smart and all, but both of you are stupid if you thought I wouldn't find out you have finally finished my work. You see these handsome young men right here on my left-hand side? These are my assassins, my spies.* He points to a group of armed men standing in the right corner.

He can't even tell his left and right!!

They are really good at their work and have been following your work for the past 4 years, right when my gut told me you were done with my project. Also, I know you have my brave soldiers working under you, but they still belong to me! You broke our contract, and it is time to pay.Your lives and life's work are now mine-the government's. Don't worry; we never planned to leave you alive after finishing my work.It was going to end the same way either way. Too bad you don't have any near relatives or a kid, because they would have joined you too. Damn, too bad! Anyway, no matter what you do right now, you aren't going to leave this building alive, so just don't try doing anything stupid, ok? Have a nice life. Oh, wait, I meant the afterlife, assuming there is one He tries laughing like a villain but rather chokes on his spit.

How can one be so incompetent!?

He takes every entry from their file and asks the mutated soldiers to follow him.

The assassins walk to the entrance of the building after the governor leaves and kill everyone who isn't willing to follow them. They kill Mr. and Mrs. Richardson after letting them watch the tragedy, and they disappear instantly.

Back to the present

John is quite after his rage. He walks back upstairs, then runs around the town, hoping to find the killer of his parents. Rather, not walking far away from the wrecked home, he finds Grandpa sitting on an ice sofa. John is surprised to see him this far away from home.

He asks Grandpa if there is a reason why he would go this far from his home. *Well, one of my young friends I befriended not too long ago lives here; he lives here.He was one of the lab rats, and this couple used to do whatever they were doing. Normally, he chats with the couple on their break, but today, just before I was about to enter these surroundings, I saw this jerk from the government with whom I have had issues before.There, I decided to stay away, but not too far away to find out what was happening inside the building. I heard and saw almost everything. I assume you have something to do with these people. Are you, by any chance, related to them? Parents or siblings of your parents? But if you are somehow their kid, then boy, you really need to leave town or the country fast! This is not a joke! Oh, I heard they never had the time to make children; forget what I just said*

John looks into his eyes and asks, *Can I trust you with something important?*

Yes of course; to me, you can tell everything. I mean, who is going to believe an old man anyway now that my brother is gone?

John smiles with pain in both eyes and continues, *Yeah, I don't know about that, but I think I can trust you. So, I am the child of the couple who ran this building. I am their son! To the outside world, I don't exist, not as part of their family.They prepared everything for my life, so nothing like this happens.My parents always told me they did it to protect something special so that one day, if something went wrong, I would be safe. To be honest, I never knew what they could've meant by „if something was to go wrong," but now I think I get it.Now that I'm seeing this, I know that nothing they ever told me or warned me about was a fairy tale or a lie. It was a real-life crisis. I know you had other reasons for coming here, but thank you very much for being here. I needed that. I would've gotten out of control one more time and killed innocent lives around this area. You are the only person here. Too much time has passed. The killers must be far gone by now, so there is no need to chase them anymore. I do know what I have to do now.I will make them pay for what they did.I will destroy their roots and make them burn in hell!I will be their reaper!!!*

Chapter 4

Grandpa tries explaining to John how absurd his plan truly is. *Hey kid, listen, it isn't that easy to go against the government. What do you think you will be able to do when you get to them? It isn't like the government is just one person sitting upstairs and controlling his country. As soon as you get one out, you will be a criminal who will be chased for the rest of his life. Worst-case scenario, they will make assassins, really bad people, chase and kill you, just like they did your parents! They are trained professionals who specialize in killing people, regardless of whether they are innocent or not. They just follow the rules.*

He takes a deep breath and continues, *You are just going to get yourself killed! Even if no one chases you, do you think you've got what it takes to end a person's life? It's not like you've ever killed anyone before; even a chicken is a problem you have to face.*

John waits for Grandpa to finish his speech and asks, *how do you know I can't kill a chicken? Whatever! You know, Grandpa, I'm not your average kid, I have an ace up my sleeves. I'm different! you know?*

Grandpa begins laughing hysterically. *I know your secret, John! I know you aren't human-not a normal human being, to be precise. You have this kind of monstrosity living within you. What did they call it again? Ahh, the Gene-Z. I already know you are mutated.*

John is surprised. He looks left and right; someone might be listening. He asks, *But how do you know? I never told you about any of this! Who are you? You seem weird - suspspiciciiously weird! Do you also work for the government? Lie, and you know what I am capable of!*

His eyes glow lightly red, and he telekinetically pulls up a sharpened rod out of the laboratory basement.

Calm down, kid! Grandpa continues, *Well, first of all, the reason why I know this is because of my friend who lived not too long ago. I assume you can figure out why I was allowed to visit him. He was a good friend of your parents and shared some secrets. He told me everything, and even if he didn't, I just saw what you did back then. Second of all, I would never work FOR the government-well, not without a good reason to benefit from it! So you want to know what I do for a living? Let's just say I tell stories; it's my gift. I am a storyteller, and I am capable of telling you as many stories as the world has to offer. Like I have lived it before! I can even tell your story. For now, I want you to live it. Listen, I know you are serious about all this, but right now, you are not the one to be going up against the government. You are too weak. Plus, the government already has some soldiers with Gene-Z. Don't worry; YOU are the real one among them for now. The others are just partly YOU because they were all born through YOU! We don't have the time for me to explain why. When the time is right, you will know; trust me!*

So what you are trying to say is...? John asks with a question-marked face.

Grandpa laughs again and tells him, *Kid, I think it is time for you to start a workout. You may have had time to train yourself at your parents' house, but I don't think it was ever enough. I also know I am capable of being a good teacher to help you find out what your true power is. I can help you master every possibility your power has to offer if you let me; I am not that bad at physics.* He winks at John.

John looks confused. He can't quite figure out why an old man could think he has what it takes to help someone as potentially powerful as him.

Does this old man have abilities like myself? It seems he has this wisdom thing; has he lived through something like this before? He doesn't seem a little bit scared, even after finding out who I am and how high my potential for changing everything is. Nahh, Johnny, you are thinking too far! He might have been a soldier in his youth or something. Maybe trusting him isn't a bad thing after all. He knows more than my parents ever did. He thinks deeply.

Kid, are you going to say something or...? You have been quiet for almost ten minutes, looking at me as if there is something you are trying to figure out. I need to know what you want, so just say yes already!

John stops daydreaming and shakes his head after coming back to the real world. He answers, *Old man, I have so many questions I have to ask you. You are giving me this kind of mystery-guy vibe. But until I have all the answers I need, I am willing to accept you as my teacher and master. It's a yes!*

Grandpa smiles after hearing his decision and tells him, *Well, whatever your questions are, I am willing to answer them. Just know, there are things I can't tell you now. Even an open book has a hidden message. We are going to train hard from now on. I am going to make you one of the most powerful beings to ever exist. First, tell me, what exactly is your ability about? What have you found out about your power? Is it an elementary power?*

John is confused, again! *What do you mean by „my actual ability" and "elementary"? I can pull and push objects like magnets or two magnets; in cartoons, they call them teli, telo, telilelokineses. It changes and gets stronger day after day. Lately, I figured out I can sense the living aura, now also the dead ones. I also remember the aura of people I have been around and connected to before my senses were activated. I don't forget easily, like a picture stuck in an album. Oh, and also the time I was angry like crazy; it felt like I was in this place-not Earth or on any other planet-I don't know, weird!*

Grandpa looks shocked and asks, *What color did you see? How long did it feel to be there?*

John thinks about what he saw while out. *Ummmmm, wait, let me think. I think the color was something orange, red, or white-ish, and I was in there for about an hour or so. I don't know, it felt like time had passed, but at the same time it was like time wasn't there, and I could move a bit. It doesn't make much sense, I know.*

Grandpa looks amazed. He draws closer and then tells him, *Kid, I think my theory about dimensions is true. Either you created a dimension by yourself or you entered one out of reach. That's amazing! We can focus on getting you there. What do you think?

Chapter 5

John has accepted Grandpa as his sensei.

What do you think, John? What is wrong? Why aren't you answering? Are you daydreaming? What is wrong? John smiles at Grandpa and tells him that there is nothing wrong with him. He was zoning out for a moment just to see what possibilities he might have in the future and what he really will be able to do once he has learned how to handle things himself. Grandpa and John begin to clean the entire house, including every laboratory. They end their clean-up by burying the corpse. Grandpa decides for John to have a funeral ceremony for his parents, just the two of them. *Johnny, kid, you shouldn't tell your parents about anything that happened today. You know exactly how it felt and what you were willing to do just because of those feelings. If you want to make this world a better place, you have to accept all this pain and endure it, like devouring all the bad food so no one will ever get to eat it. They deserve to stay healthy. Not all of them, but your parents-hell yeah! You know-sometimes caging all the pain within you is the best. It makes you stronger, so you will never be surprised when the same feelings, or maybe worse come around you. I have become really bad at giving good speeches, I think. I was once better than this trust me!Learn to see pain and anger as your fuel. The more you can hold in, the longer your strength will last.*

John tries to understand what Grandpa is trying to say, and he does. He and the old man bury all the corpses. The funeral for the last Richardsons is heartbreaking. It takes them almost the entire weekend to do so. After that, they both go back home.

At home

John does exactly what Grandpa told him to do. He talks with his parents about what could have happened, saying that they had a very nice weekend and gave him as much information as they could. His parents are happy to hear about his experience. John walks into his room with a fake smile on his face. He locks up his door and grieves. After an entire week, after all the pain-burying, he makes a big decision: he decides to change schools to a city further away. He decides to make his school route a daily workout without artificial transportation. His parents, without asking for more detail, grant him his wish and prepare everything for his new entry.

Did they find out about the tragedy? I mean, John was locked in his room for an entire week!

One year later

Every day since his school's vacation was over-the worst vacation he has ever had-John has trained for a while with his master. The time has come for him to visit his new school and decide if it is the school he wishes for.

As soon as he enters the school, he senses a strong presence.

Actually, there are two. Almost opposite sides crashed into each other, creating a new, much more powerful presence.

Woow, this aura... He is frightened by the energy.

It's stronger than mine, suppressing my will! It's like a god compared to mine!* Who is it? Is it someone like me? No, his aura's nature-it's somehow like Grandpa's-is much stronger. What happened to this person? Is it even a person? It's scary!* John is frozen. The energy is too much to handle for someone like him. *I have to get to know him and maybe be friends with him-I have to!* John decides to attend the school. It will be the school that pushes him to his limits, he thinks.

John visits Grandpa after school without going home first. He explains to him what kind of potential he sensed. Grandpa scratches his scalp.

Hmm, I knew it! he mumbles to himself. John spends the next school day walking around the school, trying to find this, though without luck. *So powerful, it's like he is everywhere!* It's P.E. time. Time for sports. John has been practicing with Grandpa how to hold back his power and now knows how to interact with normal people when it comes to power-leveling. Today in P.E. John's class, 8F, is to play with class 8D. The auras are now intensive but somehow calm-too calm to be precise. Are they here?

Dodgeball is the game today. It is fun. Class 8F is down to one player. 8D is down to two players, Lucius and Blu. John is focused on winning his first game and throws the ball harder than he needs to. Just before the ball hits Lucius, Blu gets in the way and catches it with one hand. *Wooow how coooooool! This dude is the MVP. Wooooooow, go Blu, go Blu, go Blu!!!* Every kid from 8D outside the field is jubilating. Lucius gets furious: *Why the hell did you catch my ball? It was mine, you hear me? MINE! Now stop playing my hero and give me the damn ball, bitch!* Blu laughs and tells him he was just helping out. He gives the ball to Lucius so he can make the next move. Lucius is prepared to smash the ball against John, but John is just standing there, saying nothing.

He is flabbergasted! John doesn't understand what he just witnessed. *How the hell was this dude able to catch my ball? It was more than I am allowed to throw. It was like fifteen percent more than a normal human being can throw and handle, even for a grown-up! Wait-is he the one I have been looking for? This entire time? Something doesn't seem right. He isn't showing any kind of abnormality. He is just normal. He still cannot catch something this powerful, even if he had worked out his entire body to surpass the „normal human level." His eyes! He is interesting; I need to learn more about.....* Right before thinking about his new plan to get to know him, Lucius shouts in a furious tone. *Hey, little guy, stop daydreaming and focus on me. Taste this rainbow!!!*

John screams, *oooowww!!!!*

He is hit hard and thrown a few centimeters from his standing spot. No one notices but John himself. He continues, *How the hell did it hurt so much?* and shouts, *Dude, what is wrong with you?* He starts mumbling to himself in pain, *Who are you? What are you, both of you? So there are two of you!*

I bet he is still wondering, "Who the hell are these guys?"

*They are different from other people and myself, but I don't sense any type of exposure or Gene Z in them. Wait, I also don't sense anything human on them-maybe a little, but that's it! There isn't more to it. Are they a completely new kind of mutation no soul has ever heard about? Are they some kind of newly-born gods? No, such things do not exist. Stop thinking about such a silly topic! Don't make yourself go crazy, John, come on! ... This is just a coincidence; what is the coincidence tho? Damn it. That one hurt hard! I need to be friends with them!

Shouldn't a normal person stay away from danger? This dude is crazy!

The first part of PE is over. It is time for a long break before the games continue. Everyone has left to eat, except Blu and Lucius. John is also sitting in the corner, thinking about how everything has changed while eating. Lucius isn't done with arguing about how Blu has taken away his spotlight, which will probably be his nightmare for years. *It wasn't anything special, man! It was just one single throw, and I decided to catch it so that you wouldn't have to waste your time and energy on it. Why do you have to make a big fuss out of it? I thought it would make you like me more.*

Blu smirks.

Lucius, however, isn't done yet.

Yeah, well, you thought wrong, obviously!*

He gets angrier and angrier, a state in which his emotions keep sinking, one block after the other, just like dominoes do.

You could have just stayed outta my business! I can handle myself, Mom! Fight me, and I will show you!

Blu refuses to fight Lucius. Lucius doesn't accept the refusal and attacks Blu.

They really ended up fighting! One punch after the other. Lucius' punches are as precise as those of a real boxer. This guy is good!

Even though Lucius' punches are well-aimed, he still lacks reaction time, which leads to them having an equal fight. Blu finds an opening and headlocks Lucius. The fight has almost ended. Lucius kicks his leg as hard as he can, and his shoes go up in the air, flying. A bright light flashes through their sports field, a bit further from the boys. John and the other kids, on their way back to the field, notice the fight and rush to pull them apart.

Lucius shouts and glows in a very bright white-orange-ish color.

Lucius looks glorious. What just happened?

Chapter 6

What the hell is this? It feels so strange, yet so awesome! I feel like I can do everything I want to do. Wait, I am glowing like a star, the hell? I can't move! I feel like I'm stronger, but somehow I can't move! Damn it, Blu, what the hell did you do to me? Nothing—literally nothing... I was, and I am stronger than you! Why am I only speaking inside my head? Ok, now try using your mouth like you always do. You were always good at it. Come oonn!!

A moment later...

Lucius moans, *My back hurts; it's unbearable! It feels like something is coming out of it—my glorious, beautiful back! Ngh! arghh!* He keeps shouting inside his head.

Why is no one helping me? Why are they all frozen? This isn't the time to practice your acting skills. Wait, my shoe; it has been mid-air since a while ago. Could it be that I have frozen time? Is it standing still? No, they are moving, but pretty slowly. Damn it! I don't get it. What the hell? That light is a person! How did a person flash by like that? This is impossible! Wait, me too! I am somehow impossible, like him. I mean, I can manipulate fire out of thin air, and I'm strong as fuuuuu.

The object flashing by is a man. He slowly turns his head to look at Lucius. Time is moving slowly, and the man is flashing by fast. His eyes are glowing, *just like Blu's eyes. Just, Blu's eyes glow pure bluuueee... waaaaiiiit a minute. B-L-U...* he begins to spell, *and his eyes glow B-L-U-E.*

Lucius is noticing something about his comrade.

Are you kidding me!?! Wait, focus! This one's eyes are glowing white-ish; there is more to it. They aren't glowing the same color. Is he a god, like the Monkey King? I feel so different than I normally do. It is like being around Blu, or at least how it feels when he activates his powers. That bastard! Damn it! I am thinking about how damn cool he can be in this kind of situation!? It makes me feel angrier than I already am right now. Hey, awesome ass dude. I know you probably can't hear me right now. Who the hell are you, and where do you come from? Ugh Whatever, Just help me, Geesh!!

The glowing man starts moving towards Lucius and places his index finger on his lips. Lucius should remain calm. He stands in front of Lucius and holds onto his shoulders. Lucius' glowing begins to fade. His vision becomes clear enough for him to partially see the stranger's face. His fingers begin to twitch.

Let's jump back ages before...

Lucius is born into a normal family. His father is a doctor, and his mother is a college teacher. During the first few days after his birth, everything seemed normal. How he acts, how he smiles, how he shouts out, crying as a baby boy... He learns to talk, much earlier than any baby would.

At the age of two, he starts showing some signs of abnormality. Every time his mother tries to give him a drink, he always refuses to drink. Each time, the cup vibrates lightly for a few seconds, almost unrecognizable, at least for his mother. This keeps going on and becomes more recognizable as he grows up and gets stronger.

On his ninth birthday, his mother, knowing her son hates tomato juice, gives him a big bottle of it as a gift. Lucius, without hesitation, squeezes the bottle without needing to touch it. He squeezes as hard as possible until it reaches the highest pressure and bursts, spraying everyone in the room with red, sweet, and tomato juice.

His mother finally figures out that her son isn't that normal after all. He is a freak!

But he is still my son, and I still love him, she says.

She blames herself for trying to pull a prank on him every single year with the same prank, which never ends well. It is all her fault for making him like this. A few days after the birthday, she decides to have a mother-son day with her son.

Lucius, I have a story to tell you. It is much like a family history that was supposed to be buried a long time ago. Just listen to what I am going to tell you. No matter what path you choose after that, I will always support you!

Chapter 7

Mama Lucius finds a spot to sit with her son, right in the middle of the woods. Lucius tells her how and why this exact spot is his favorite. His mother nods her head and tells him she has known it already and that she knows a lot about what Lucius has experienced.

Lucius, you see, I know a lot about everything happening. It was a feeling I always had. Hanging out with someone makes it possible for me to know things about them, mostly precious things. I am still considered normal though.

a normal?, Lucius hears these exact words for the first time from his mother.

She continues...

Normal means a normal human being. My parents said my abilities were "just" something normal. something like intuition. She said this because, in the past, those were about him. I don't know exactly who He is, but He seems to play an important role in our family history. His story goes like this:

Long ago In the old ages, when gods used to live on the same ground as us human beings, the weaker ones, being humankind, were slaves to the superior ones. The gods created everything around them. Even though men weren't able to see them, they always believed in the messenger's sayings about the world under their control.

Some gods disguised themselves as men and paired with mankind. Willingly or not, they bore beautiful half-gods who were much stronger than the average human. This happened over centuries, until one day an unknown god showed up. He was really strong and powerful; he even showed his face and how he was able to create life. He was called the Monkey King. Though he never looked like a monkey. He just explained that his name was given to him by his best friend because of his animalistic character and his movements, just like a monkey but more elegant. He was the embodiment of every creature created, and he made his people feel comfortable around him. He told stories about what needed to happen in the future and that everything had to happen in a specific time period. He disappeared and appeared as time went by, just as he had always promised his people. Every time he reappeared, it was at the same time that his people needed him the most.

He reproduced with human beings, just like other gods did. He explained that his reproduction wasn't to make more slaves but to make them capable of fighting stronger beings like him to protect men.In wars created by the gods, he was always there and fought with his sons. Even though they lost many battles, they still proved their strength and got stronger after every battle.

In every third generation, there was always a descendant who was claimed to be the strongest of them all. He is even stronger than the father of the strongest demigods, they assumed, though no one was sure how strong he was. The last war he fought was called the War of the Titans. The name was given by one of the Monkey King's followers. The goal was to erase everything and everyone, just to create new people who were less evolved and not willing to stand against the gods. The Monkey King knew this day would come, creating a counterplan-a plan he had been working on for ions.

The War of the Titans was the deadliest war known to mankind. It was the first between gods and creation. Though the story was forgotten throughout time, its existence is still preserved by victimized families, all descendants of the Monkey King.

Around eighty percent of his sons were forever gone. He was completely weakened in this war; it was impossible to try and make more children. The remaining members of his bloodline were girls and women who were strong, loving, and gifted with abilities. Some were called magicians and healers. After losing their real names, they were later called witches. People feared their existence and found a way to end their lives.

Before the Monkey King disappeared for the last time, he promised to reappear and walk Earth till the end of time, once the strongest generation of his bloodline was born. A generation so strong will be considered gods with almost no limit in power.

"The time shall come in which my children will become stronger than all and find what I never could. They will hate and love each other. Their love will change their destiny, and

I will fight among them. Let them know who I am when the time comes. Until then, you shall keep silent and hurt no soul."

In every generation, there was always a new story told about the Monkey King. Pyramids were perfected, gravitational equations were discovered, math became a subject with no limits known to humankind, it evolved to a discovery that was called physics, electricity was discovered, the light bulb and a new cult, the government, were invented, exactly as he prophecised.Jamie, Lucius' ancestor, was the first, after many generations of his family, to be a male demi-god. His family feared him. He was both kind and furious. He had everything a leader should have. His power was beyond imagination. He could create and destroy without breaking a sweat. He was the god of his time. His best friend, who was mostly hidden behind his shadow, grew older and became almost as strong as him. Everyone had hope.

"The Monkey King will be walking among us soon!" they thought.

Those who knew about the legend's truth tried spreading the news to other family members. They sang and rejoiced for years, but the monkey king never returned.

"He let us down; he forgot about us," they began saying with sad voices. Jamie knew he wasn't the promised descendant. He and his friend grew much stronger.

"Maybe if we become much stronger than we are right now, we might be able to bring him back and put a smile on everyone's lips." They traveled around the world to see and understand everything there was.

After living for one hundred and thirty-nine years, Jamie's best friend began having suicidal thoughts. He wasn't willing to live much longer on Earth. Jamie tried showing him how life could be beautiful if only they were able to become as strong as needed. His plan worked; his best friend was willing to live, but he also wanted to be the only one to succeed. He worked on a plot for a hundred more years. He founded the first government to ever exist and showed his followers Jamie's devilish side. The government decided to eliminate him, threatening to kill his family unless he turned himself in.

At the age of 241, Jamie had to turn himself in. Many relatives were killed, even though the government promised to let them go after Jamie had turned himself in. The only survivors were the non-believers of the family who traveled abroad to live their lives, far away from the drama behind the Monkey King. Jamie said his last goodbyes to an entire crowd watching his execution. He was burned in the sunlight with blue flames. It was never known how many blue flames were created, and no one bothered to ask questions.

His death left the family with female mutants. Their presence was very weak, weaker than every female mutant to ever exist; therefore, the last option was to remain hidden. The non-believers among the relatives abroad heard about the execution. They started to believe in something beyond understanding; they were made believers. His death was like a curse upon all descendants of the Monkey King. The survivors were too weak to spread their stories and defend themselves; every generation only had one mutant, and the families began hating each other as there was no order as to which family would have the next mutant.

Lucius' great-grandmother was the last one known to be mutated in his family. Now it is Lucius. Something doesn't seem right. This time, there is more than just one. Something has changed, but what exactly? The others are yet to be found.*

Lucius' mom and another woman somewhere else say the same words at the same time:

*That's all I know about our family, Lucius.**That is all I know about our family, Blu.*

Mama Lucius adds, *There might be more to know, but I think you will know when the time is right. You might be among the prophecy's strongest generation. I have the feeling you aren't the only one. It feels like somehow our curse has been broken. I feel multiple you...s, and they are much closer than ever. Maybe you should find them and grow stronger together, no matter what happens. Show the world your burning flames!* She touches her hurt chest. Lucius believes in everything. He has been sensing another person, somehow calm but also with a strong presence. He decides to change his class.

He is calling me; I am sure he is in this class.

We all know who this second person is now, don't we?

Chapter 8

Lucius' entire life has been a bit of everything. Painful, held together, messy, alone, with love, with hate... After discovering he can move objects telekinetically, he decides to find out more about his powers.

He has used his boring free time since childhood for stories; reading is his hobby. His favorite genres are history, gods, fictional stories, and almost everything about impossibilities and superhuman powers. He has also spent more time with his mother, ever since she told him about his family history.

He and his parents have decided to keep what makes him special a secret. His mother, together with Lucius, finds out about his flames-hot, red, scary flames.

They manifested out of nothing. It isn't something one would imagine a child having

He has had a hard time controlling the nature of fire and keeps burning parts of his body every time he tries holding up the flames for more than a minute. *It doesn't even make sense! Why do I get burned by the flames my body produces? Mama, am I cursed?* He asks his mother these questions several times.

Mama Lucius refuses to think deeper into it to give her son an answer. She decides to spill a secret she has been holding for a while after a dangerous incident-a secret that has been bothering her for a while. She tells him, *There is one man who also knew about our family history. It might sound crazy, but even though he should have been dead by now, I have the feeling he is among us, watching every step we take. He was an old storyteller who always told us he would be forever young and immortal. He never looked as young as he claimed to be and also not as old as he believed to be-a weird man! His stories were really fun and interesting, but the man himself was never my personal favorite. His stories were like a real-life experience, like he had lived it. Sometimes I had the feeling he was talking about something that was going to happen soon. He named one of his characters after me. She said she would marry Nathaniel.*

Wait, but dad is called Nathaniel?, Lucius puts the pieces together. Her only answer is a "yes," while a shiver runs down her spine.

She continues, *It's like I knew everything but always forgot until it happened. Even you-your name. He said exactly when and where you would be born and what your name would be. I noted the name for the future, so I wouldn't use it. Your dad and I were going to decide what your name would be after you were born, but I went into deep sleep after you came out. I woke up weeks later and then heard...*

*My name had already been chosen, and it was Lucius, just like he said. * Lucius gets where it's all going. "Yes!" is once again her short answer, looking more concerned than ever.

He said you were the devil's new. I still don't understand what he meant by that. We might find out about that one day. One more thing... I am pretty familiar with the old stories about our ancestors, and I sometimes noticed these strange relics from the past-relics that should have stayed there or with the family

His mom's stories make him giddy. The stories never scare him off at all; rather, they make him yearn for more. A part of him never wants to believe anything is real. He keeps explaining to his mother how such events couldn't take place in real life.

"No human being can live for that long!" Is always his answer. *There is no such thing, Mom! I think you were just putting some fake pieces of a story together because his presence was frightening you. Do you think he is like me? If he is, then he can't live for so long. See, I keep aging, just like a normal person*; he argues.

Eventually, he caves in and accepts all the facts. *Well, it's not impossible tho, Mama. If what you keep saying is true, it would mean Grandpa Jamie was over two hundred years old, and his appearance never looked like he was that old. How did no one notice it?* A new mystery is created for a new detective.

His mother explains the fact that she and Aunt June are the only ones to remember such things about him. Everyone has forgotten many details in his story.

They remember these as if they were there themselves, as if they were Jamie himself. *It's like a backed-up video of everything he had, was, and remembered. It's like he trusted us to preserve his existence.* They decided to keep the information to themselves, as every close family member never knew a thing, and no one would ever believe them. Everyone either has the memory of him living a normal life and bringing hope to the family, or there is no memory left of his existence.

Many remember a few pieces that aren't easy to put together. Though their story is almost completely accurate, it ended up having a different interpretation. They mixed it up with another man's life and named it the story of Jesus. They believed the story took place two thousand years ago.

Now there are two stories about Jesus, and no one can tell which one is the real one or mixed up.

Though I somehow have the feeling he is still alive, that man should be dead by now. Maybe he never really existed, and it was some kind of prophecy I had been daydreaming about.

Lucius understands what his mom is trying to tell him. He shouldn't get the idea of looking for someone whose existence was never proven. He frowns a little and scrumps his nose after making sure his mom knows he is going to let the topic stay a fairy tale.

Young Lucius kept in mind that there were dangerous things that he could encounter at any time in his life. Every day after school, he spent his time training his abilities, both fire and telekineses, and got a bit stronger every day.

His mother teaches him to meditate. After a few lessons, it becomes part of the daily routine. They have fun together. He is told to make every negative emotion coursing through his head flow out during meditation, as he has a rather terrifying temper.

One Saturday, Lucius' mom decides to meditate with him for a double amount of time. Lucius is fully motivated and gives his best. His mother pulls him away from reality, making him fantasize on his own.

This time, he isn't going to flush away negative emotions.

Try combining every emotion and pulling them all out; everything that was gone needs to be drawn back-all at the same time. You need to feel everything at once, think of something to contain them while they're there, and create something new-something you want. While doing so, show me every single thing you hate and what you love. Balance your emotions and use them as fuel; they have to be burned after we are done today. She whispers in his ears.

She pulls back again.

She raises her voice just a bit so he doesn't lose her and tells him, *First, start imagining yourself in a self-made garden and then pull someone you want to meet in it, me!

Lucius searches for a specific person, not his mother. He gets to see a silhouette for a split second. He pushes himself harder.

His mother opens her eyes. She thinks that her son has pulled her in; rather, she sees something strange: Lucius is Levitating and every light-weighted object is flying around him in a circle, almost like a heavy storm indoors.

His mother wants to call off the meditation. Lucius, however, doesn't respond.

She goes back to meditating, trying hard to somehow find a connection to him. Right as she concentrates on her son, Lucius thinks about her and pulls her in. She feels him pull and opens her eyes.

She is sure that it isn't the real world she is in. She walks around to find him.

Why did Lucius choose something like this?, she murmurs to herself. His reality is warm. It feels like one is wanted in there, but at the same time, the reality is hot and trying to drag you out. A simultaneous push and pull with something electric-current-like rushing through the entire body in every direction possible.

Imagine that at one point you are somewhere, and at the same time you aren't. It's hard to imagine, isn't it?

Chapter 9

An hour has passed in the real world since Lucius' mother has been searching. There are still no signs of him.

In the real world...

Lucius' mother is levitating, just like she saw Lucius do. A mixture of white and dark smoke is flowing out of her pants and blouse. Is something burning? Is it her? Her clothes? Or is Lucius doing something to her without realizing it himself?

Her husband rushes down the stairs after smelling something burning in the living room. He sees his wife and son sitting facing each other. He sees his wife partly covered in black and white smoke. She turns over to Lucius, just to see white smoke underneath his breath. Lucius takes a deep breath. Smoke comes out of his nose, mouth and ears.

His father, not knowing what exactly is happening, is panicking; he doesn't know what to do in this situation. He clears his throat and takes a deep breath as he draws back out of the smoke.

He picks up the towel underneath his wife and covers his nose with it. While pressing it on his face, he lightly slaps his wife.

Hey, can you hear me? What is happening to you two? Are you alright? Say something! Honey-pie, please tell me you guys have this under control! Is this what you meant by the history of your family? I thought you were a normal person! Isn't that what you told me?

He raises his voice and shouts in agony, *Wake up? How are you flying, and what the hell is happening?!*

He lowers his voice as he begins crying for their sake. He continues, *I thought it was all just a story you wanted to tell. I should have believed you. Now I do, so just stop what you are doing and come back, please!* He whispers under his breath, *I have a bad feeling about this!*

He tries touching his wife's face once more. Her body is so hot, he burns his palm.

She is literally boiling!

Both Lucius and his mother are hot, and the room has dropped from thirty degrees Celsius to room temperature, twenty degrees Celsius. Lucius' father discovers this after checking the thermometer. He is wondering how it is possible. It is summer, and the room should be almost as hot as outside. Instead, the room's temperature has dropped rapidly, like an a.c. Wait, like an A.C.! The medium becomes hot as the room gets colder.*

It takes him a while to remember something he has seen in an action movie. He continues murmuring to himself, *Could it be that my wife does have superpowers after all and is absorbing all the unnecessary heat in the room? But even so, why is she hovering off the ground with Lucius? Does she have multiple abilities? Nah, I don't think so. This would mean the other ability comes from my son. I would like to say that I am proud, but to be honest, I don't even know the right thing to do.*

Two hours have passed in the real world since Lucius' mother exited it. For her, she has been gone for almost twenty minutes.

Three hours have passed in the real world, and they are still not back...

Four hours in, and they're still not back...

Lucius' eyes are starting to glow blue with flaming red sparks. His father is terrified by the change. He tries to remain calm and continues watching them.

There isn't something I can do now, is it?, he asks himself.

Calling the police or ambulance won't even work. They will just end up being more confused than I am right now.

He grabs himself a big glass of coffee and a second one filled to the brim with red wine. * I am going to keep myself awake to support you guys, whatever you are doing. I don't even get why I keep talking to you; you can't even hear what I am saying.

Inside the created reality...

Mama Lucius is still searching for her son after an hour away from her location. She continues shouting out his name, *Luci boy!*

Maybe he will hear me and follow my voice, she thinks. She has a powerful voice. Standing in her range of movement can shake one's insides. Even the deaf will feel more than her vocal vibration.

One might say it will make a deaf person understand her words, even though it isn't the loudest she has to offer. *Dude!*, She sighs deeply and continues walking.

I have the feeling this isn't just a planet he is imagining. The sky also looks weird, or maybe not? There is neither sun nor star, just red skies. Is time different here? Faster or slower? What is happening in the real world with our bodies? I hope the storm has stopped making a mess inside our living room. I am not motivated at all to clean up again. I just did the cleaning last night. Geezesus, Lucius, show yourself! Please? I want to go back. I don't feel well. I'm getting dizzy! I feel my chest weight heating up. They are burning up from the inside, she says.

She tumbles and falls slowly to the ground. She looks up to the sky and wonders, *That is weird! Did I fall in slow motion? I thought it was going to hurt—like a lot!*

She manages to stand up but falls once more. Her legs are weakened. She feels her energy being sucked up slowly by an unknown source. She is unable to get back on her feet and decides to stay down for a while until she has recovered enough to be able to stand up again.

She uses her last strength to raise both her arms and sees something scary: her arms are thinner, and her entire body is thinner than it was before she was pulled in.

So my power was being drained this entire time, huh? I give up...

Just before she loses every last ounce of motivation, she hears someone shouting out her name, *Mom, Mom... Mom!!! Wake up!*

A smile brightens up her face while she whispers, *Lucius, is it you?* Her voice has almost faded away.

Lucius rushes to her and apologizes. He realizes his mother is unable to survive in his reality and tells her how and why she isn't supposed to be there. He calms her down and touches her forehead. His mother's temperature drops rapidly. She can stand back up. As for her blouse, it is burning from her chest outward.

Lucius tells her with sadness in his voice, *Mom, you aren't supposed to be here. Without my help, it would be hell for someone like you. Go back and wait for me. And now... RETURN!!* He pushes her consciousness out of his world and starts to search for someone to give him answers.

His mom is weakened in the real world and needs to rest. Her chest is glowing red. Her heart had been heated the entire time.

What does it mean?

Lucius starts meditating in his spiritual reality and shouts, *Monkey King, I know you can hear me; show yourself!!!*

Chapter 10

* Hey, Nathan, Simon, wake up! Do you see that light over there? Do you see it? Is it an angel? No, it looks like a person!

Nathan looks confused and asks, *Jin, what are you talking about?* He turns around to double-check their cell and adds, *There is nothing there apart from our shoes! Are you kidding, or has craziness already caught up to you? You've only been in this cell with us for ten years already. I think you are getting cra - zy!* He points his finger right above his right ear and starts twirling his index finger.

Simon, the most chilled one out of the three, wakes up, turns his head in Jin's direction, and starts talking to him, right after a huge sigh, *Listen, Jin, we know you are two months longer in here than us but still, dude, get a hold of yourself! You only have five more years in here - well, assuming they finally find the man who killed your sister.*

Jin panics. He says, *Yo, Hey! I'm not joking; it's coming closer!*

Don't bother; they can't hear you anymore; they also can't see me or hear me. Right now, it's just you and me. Master and father of the outcasts. It's time to wake up and awaken, the beginning of the end of a beginning needs to start now! You have been resting for far too long. I have been waiting for you to call upon me this entire time.

I never called you Jin says. He thinks about not continuing the conversation.

After a short silence, he still does. He walks towards him and touches the edge of his nose with his index finger. He says, *I don't even know who or what you are! What do you want from me? And also... why are you talking to me like that? It's kinda weird. You are kinda weird!* He asks again, *Who or what the hell are you?*

It is me, Michael-Mikey, Michael-Silvester! You told me to find you and help reset something about your timeline. Well, your words were exactly, "The day shall come in which my younger presence shall look for help out of a situation. The day shall be in the far future, and I will look much less than I do right now. Because of me being nothing, it shall be nearly impossible to find me. I shall be weak and worthless, but a genius. I shall be less wise and not know you. Be patient with me till I begin to trust you. Until the day comes, you shall be cursed with my abilities and live eternally. The day shall come, and you shall tell me these exact words. Remember them!" Sooo, all you need to do is accept your awakening so I can have a normal life with normal abilities. I don't need to be that much of a powerful demi-god.

Wait, a demi-god? What are you talking about, man? Jin is more confused.

Listen, you are my father, ok? You are the real god, he says, showing original features without a literal glow-up.

Before I was able to awaken my powers, you cast a curse upon me. I would walk the earth until it was time for you to be awakened.It was selfish of you, but you may have had good reasons to do so. I think I finally understand how this all works. It means you are a normal human being who gets a gift-in this case, he gifts himself with abilities that he eventually awakens to be able to live longer than a person. Otherwise, you should have your powers right now. But you still had them after you cursed me; now you are just powerless like every normal human being. That one I don't get yet. Anyway, you told me I would be able to decide if I wanted to awaken my inner god or live a normal life with a means to an end, and that either way, I would have the ending I always wished for.Just please take back your powers before we discuss further issues. I have lost so many loved ones that I can't do this anymore. Hold both my hands and say after me, „Meha mi no seikan no Tomie me sine - nin"

Jin looks into the eyes of the man. Somehow, he believes every single word and is sorry for everything that has happened to him. He holds his hands and repeats, *Meha mi no seikan no Tomie me sine... ni! Did I say it riiiiggghhh.. ooooooohhhhhh.. hooooooooly...* He starts burning up.

Both him and his self-proclaimed son are captured by a strong void filled with fire and blue lightning, and in between them are particles of the deepest darkness. A thunderstorm strikes their position. A pile of smoke appears through the lightning strike. They are sucked into the void and disappear from the prison cell. Nathan and Simon notice him flash for a second and pull back.

Both Nathan and Simon shout with their highest pitch, like a little girl.

Simon asks, *Wait, what the hell just happened? What..*, Nathan ends the question, * the? *

JIn?

Inside the void...

Jin and his companion are floating through the void. He holds his stomach as tight as he can and says, *H-hey, y-you, what was your name again? What in heaven's name is happening right now? I don't feel so-so good. I think I have to pu.. urgh* he pukes into the nothingness.

His puke is filled with half-chewed pieces of carrots and a white-green-colored liquid.

*Ugh, that tastes awful! I think I'm good. Noow, oh sh*t! Urgh* Once again, he pukes, this time even more than the first.

Could you just stop puking? Jeez! You are such a baby, and my name is Silvester, he claims.

Jin laughs, *Oh wait, let me just tell my body to stop being affected by something it has never felt before!*

Please do it faster! Wait, is it possible? Jin gives him a judgmental look and shouts, *No, of course not, double-stein! What do you think?*

Double-stein: a mockery reference to Einstein...

Silvester isn't troubled by Jin's answers. He gives him an unexpected answer; *I think a god should be able to do such an easy task.*

What do you mean by that? Who said I was a god?

Did Jin forget everything Silvester told him?

Jin doesn't understand what is going on. Jin sits with his legs folded underneath his body.

Though he is sitting upside down, from Jin's perspective

Silvester sighs, *It seems like you don't know anything about yourself - your past self. I have the feeling that this is where your origin story begins, so your past self might be a different future for you? Alright, for starters... Do you get it? Starters because this is the start, like the beginning? You don't?*

Jin isn't answering; instead, he stares blankly into his face.

Silvester continues, *Alright, well, you are my father; I have told you before, and it seems this is the point where your life begins. I have studied a little bit about how time flows and what it feels like to make the loop continue.You will, at some point in time, curse my younger self to make the story go on. Meaning, if you hadn't taken my hand at the exact moment you did and we hadn't taken this path we are on, at the same time, even though time doesn't affect us here, the timeline in which I lived until now would cease to exist.I have witnessed others challenging time, and been evaporated by it. Meaning, I would evaporate in front of your eyes, and you may or may not have remembered what had happened. You seem to be one of the gods who awakened as soon as they got hold of their powers, though I do have the feeling, you aren't completely awakened. Something big is going to happen very soon. I assume we will be back in the present as soon as it begins. I will finally be able to live freely. You will have to take me back if you plan to stay longer. I don't have the ability to travel through a time void.*

Jin's eyes widen.

Daaaaaaamn, son, you gooooood! It seems like I taught you very well. So what you mean is that I am a god, and from the looks of it, I'll be the only god to live among men. So for the people, I will be the only god that has ever existed, with living proof. Alright, let's go start our own story. Call me the Monkey King, the one history books talk about. I will make those legends come true!

Chapter 11

Somewhere in BC, before time became important...
Jin and Silvester are out of the void. Their first adventure has ended.

now...

The second begins...

They arrive in an empty cave in Heliopolis, an ancient kingdom on continent C.

It is really hot here, Jin cries out loud. He isn't a fan of warm, hot surroundings.

Currently, they don't know where exactly they are. All they know is... they just jumped through a void and ended up in a cave, a massive cave, the largest cave in the world!

They walk towards the exit of the cave, which they believe to be the exit from the cave to the outside world. *Dad, how do you know this path is towards the exit?* Silvester asks. Jin starts smiling. He widens his smile and laughs out loud as he tells his son. * To be honest, I don't know man, but... I think we arrived in Anthopia—what did they call it in the past? Egypt?* He asks rhetorically and answers, *Yes, that's the original name, right?*

He continues, *Well, it would mean the path with larger rocks leads outside this cave. I feel like this is the capital city of Anthopia, Heliopolis. Judging from how young these rocks look, we traveled through time, and we are a few years after their official discovery. So this is the ancient Heliopolis, huh? Never been there personally. It is known to be the lost cave. Though there is an entrance, no one has been able to enter and find out its secrets, not in the future. Being inside here means it was never always like that. However, I have seen these cave drawings somewhere before.*

He thinks for a while...

They seem a bit different from what I tried studying a couple of years ago—or, should I rather say, many years in the future? hahaha He laughs at his joke while Silvester hits his forehead, shaking his head, questioning how someone like his father is considered smart.

Jin goes back to being serious. He says, *I understand almost half of what is written here.*

Meanwhile, Silvester gets excited and curious. He asks Jin, *What do the symbols say?* He is surprised by what his dad has achieved during his lifetime.

Jin jumps back and forth from one symbol to the next; the symbols aren't read in "correct, normal order." His face and ears glow slightly red. The redness of his face can be seen through his light, almost darkened skin.

This is a treasure house, man! It feels like I can learn more and more about history. These people write about their most important adventures. Why does this one say one was killed while he was taking the largest dump in history? No, he murdered his own ass, hahaha. Oh wait, here it says to keep the information for one's self, "Only thou soul, worthy to understand us, shall keep our saying." Sorry, man, I would like to tell you more, but a rule is a rule, boy!

He sighs loudly. *F'ck it, people will eventually reveal the meaning of these symbols in the future anyway, so what the hell? Alright, most of them say how much the people have missed their protectors, the gods. The language spoken between the gods and the people is almost forgotten. In their time, when they wrote all these, half of the followers couldn't translate well. Those who did tried translating their language into new symbols, which were easier to translate. They wanted their future generations to be able to read it; there are thirty-nine different kinds of symbol languages.*

His son adds, *So it means there is a superior language that no one can understand, and it translates into thirty-nine?*

Jin isn't surprised; it is easy to understand what he just explained; therefore, Silvester has only underlined and shortened what he just said.

He answers with "exactly" and continues translating, *It says many things about how they were protected and also that they loved their lives as they lived underneath the gods. Wait, they loved and worshipped them, even though the gods treated them like shit! They were like slaves to the gods and thought it was the price they had to pay to be protected from negativity—but the gods made negativity! It sounds like an awful story!*

Silvester listens quietly as his father tells him everything about the cave stories.

It is starting to get brighter as they walk further. Silvester doesn't need to light up the walls for his father. Jin finds something interesting. *It says here that the latest language invented is similar to the second translation of the first language, the ancient language. They call it hieroglyphs. "The reader of one of the two languages needs to be careful after mastering both languages. Though they look similar and seem to have the same meaning, hieroglyphs are the simple version of the ancient language, making it lose a lot of important details, depending on the situation." Silvester, do you know what this means? I could have misread many things; the one with the dump murder has to be it! The symbols are simple, and to be honest, I can't imagine the stories going differently than what I read...*

Shhhhhht! Jin shushes Silvester. *Something is coming towards us really fast. How am I able to hear and feel something that is so far away? Is it part of my ability? It's super fast. It can't be a human, but it is! It is powerful; it has to be a man! Wait, is this also part of my ability to sense threats?*

Father Jin is happy about his ability. He is frightened to meet whatever is coming towards them. They have slightly walked past an intersection, and the object is nearer than before. *He should be here in a minute!*

He pulls Silvester back, and they take a different path. *It's a dead end!* Silvester informs.

The path has rocks of many sizes stacked upon each other. Jin throws himself against the rocks, thinking he is strong enough to push them out of his way. He needs to take that exact path if he wants to get out without facing the object.

Instead of hitting the rocks with as much strength as he has to offer, he phases through them.

He is gone...

Hello? Dad? What the hell just happened? Did he just float through these solid rocks? Silvester tries punching the rocks to be sure they are solid. *Of course, they were solid, and it hurts bad!*

He moves backwards and hits something hard. *Huh?*

A man is standing behind him. He is well-built and seems to be strong enough to beat him in a fight. *Who are you, and what are you doing here? You are not one of us! Who sent you? Was it my father? Is he trying to punish us again?* The stranger asks Silvester with a furious look on his face.

Silvester is confused.

Umm well, hi, I'm Silvester. Yes, I'm a stranger, and yes, that means I'm not one of your people. I don't even know who your father is. Would you mind enlightening me?

The stranger raises his right eyebrow and says, *You, stranger, do speak awkwardly, but I do process everything you have tried saying to me. Do not fear, for I shall reveal to you who I am and who my father is. I am willing to fulfill your wish and enlighten you about what you have asked.*

He sits on the ground and adds, *My father is known as one of the god-fathers; you cannot not know him; he goes by the name Zeus.*

Silvester gives him a serious look and asks, *Zeus' son? For real? Wait, are we not in Antho, I mean Egypt, right now?* His serious look becomes more intense.

The son of Zeus tells him that his younger brother, who might as well be one of the strongest to exist among the demi-gods, is sent to find him, kill him, and everything attached to him, meaning his entire family, clan, and maybe even all of Greece. He has traveled all the way to Egypt. The gods of Egypt have been gone for a while now, and he protects them in exchange for keeping his identity a secret.

Silvester can't believe he is with Zeus' son, his half-human son. *I thought that Zeus' sons were always around him? Are you really Zeus' son? Holy...!* They both sense a powerful presence moving towards them.

That is not my Father Jin, and... why am I even sensing someone getting closer? It shouldn't be possible since I gave away my father's curse! He is questioning everything that is happening at the moment.

Jin phases through the rocks, back to his son.

Who the hell are you? Let me guess, some kind of god?, he asks. Zeus' son looks at him with wide-opened eyes, and he answers, *As I see, you have been gifted with wisdom. Without ever having spoken to me, you guessed who I am. This man here does not work with my father. Seeing your similarities brings me to the conclusion that you do belong together. Are you perhaps Father Jin? And what attributes of mine sold me out?*

Jin smiles, then laughs; he can't contain the urge to laugh louder. He replies, *Well, for starters, look at how you are dressed, all in white, and then there is this scarf tied around your head and stuff, your eyes glowing blue, white... ish. Maybe next time try hiding yourself; it doesn't seem like you were good at it. Oh, and also, you've gotta stop wearing that dress, hahaha. Alright, let's leave now. Something is coming, with negative emotions, rage, and anger. We will die if it catches up to us here in this cave. Question, why do you speak so weirdly?*

Chapter 12

Jin, Silvester, and the son of Zeus have been rushing out as quickly as they can for the past two minutes.

Right before they reach the exit...

Jin asks the stranger for his name. He answers, *Morphius is the name given to me, and thus shall be the name you will be allowed to call me.*

Jin sighs loudly, again. He sighs one last time-a long sigh. He eventually starts laughing and tells Morphius, that his way of speaking is ridiculous.

He stops running and shouts at Morphius, asking him, *Hey, you! You claim to be the son of Zeus, but I haven't ever heard of him having a son named Morphius. So are you going to tell me what your lie is all about? Start by telling us who you really are!*

Morphius is confused, *I do not lie and don't intend to do such a disgust! I am the firstborn of Zeus. Also, I am the first demi-god ever to walk on this fertile ground. My existence was to be kept from every living thing. My father himself never had the honor to meet me, nor was he ever told he had a son half-descending from his slaves. My mother suffered an eternity of her life, keeping me hidden for as long as she could, but at some point Zeus, as smart as he is, found out about me. I am much older than I look. All a mortal son like yourself should know is that I am almost twice as old as a normal being should be. My flesh doesn't age fast enough to make my age noticeable. I am running from my brother, the well-known brother, Ares. He has killed most of my siblings. Perseus and I, Morphius, seem to be the last ones he hasn't killed yet. I think Perseus is still alive because he has been kept safe by my father; it is more like he is pretending not to know him. He now goes by Percy Jackson.*

Jin is surprised. *So that's why history never talked about you. You aren't supposed to exist, ever!*

He starts moving and continues, *Even if so, it seems like you will be killed before any man finds out who you are and that you are really important to history-not really to history, but whatever, I guess? So our first enemy is Ares, huh? He must be really powerful. I think I can take him on. He doesn't bring me out of my comfort zone. It will be hard to break him down, though.*

Morphius laughs as Jin talks about his plan to take down Ares. Jin isn't happy about him laughing as loud as he is and asks him what is funny about anything he is saying.

Morphius answers, *Mortal man, I do not think that you have the gift to be strong enough to face my brother. Even I, his brother of the same blood, and my siblings, may they rest in peace, will never reach his power. Both you and this man here are going to die if you stay with me! He should be here any moment now. You mentioned something important;

what do you mean by history and that no one will know m...*

Right before finishing his question, he gets hit in the tummy with a powerful punch. *uurrghhh!!!* The wielder of the punch drags him away from Jin and Silvester, hitting the cave walls. Jin isn't impressed by the power and speed behind the overwhelming presence. His head is still facing Morphius' recent location, while his eyes are following Morphius as he gets pulled away.

huh, he whispers. *Well, I have to admit, this dude is really powerful, damn! Just look at how a god's son was blown away with just one strike. Hey you! I'm guessing you are Ares or whatever. What is your issue with this dude? And why are you killing all your siblings? Answer me!*

Ares quickly turns around and looks at Jin. He breathes out powerfully and asks, *Who are you, and how does a mortal man like yourself know who and what I am? How dare you command me?! You pathetic creatures are meant to know your place and kneel before a powerful presence like mine! Your bravery to talk upon me shall be rewarded right before your life is taken out of this world. My father, the almighty, powerful Zeus, trained me to be one of the strongest warriors known to man! I am the strongest child, and I intend to prove it to all. I find peace in taking what I want and destroying everything beneath me, trying to put itself above me. Father was once mad about my behavior, killing his „beloved beings." He imprisoned me for that, instead of being proud to have a son like I am. Eventually, he gave up after finding out he had a son, a demi-god who lived alongside his playthings. He found out his "first son" wasn't the first after all. He set me free and asked me to find out who this child was disguised as. "Find him and then break him!" were his words. Well, with break, he always means killing, just so you lower creatures know what someone as mighty as us is speaking of. I was mad, really mad. He imprisons me for an eternity and commands me to do his bidding. I wanted to pay him back, but I did not know how. My siblings tried stopping me, believing the imposter would grow up to be mighty. They thought he would become strong enough to face our father and rebuild the relationship between us gods and the lower beings. As for me, I do not let anyone tell me what to do, except sometimes my father, because... yeah, so I killed them all, returning them to the ashes. They are now spending their non-existence in the chaos of existence.*

He walks towards Jin and stretches his arms, showing his presence and dominating the atmosphere. He says, *I have no fun killing lower beings like you without you having the chance to beg for mercy. I will give you two suns. Run as fast as you can and never look back.

He turns around and looks at his brother. He changes his mind and says, *Maybe I should let my brother in on this deal, but I think he might be fast enough to make it harder for me. Whatever, it is more fun to see all the fear in his eyes after I find him.*

He looks up and takes a deep breath.

Mhhhh, it will be refreshing. I am going to have fun breaking you all apart. He will finally find his place in the beloved chaos. As for you, I do not know where your final destination will be. You are of no meaning to the existence of chaos. I will finally head back home and enjoy myself. Or maybe, I will try getting stronger, stronger than my father and then kill him. Will it be to my satisfaction? Or do I just destroy the realm of the gods? Before you run for your lives, Answer me this. What and who are you? You are not from this world, strangers! I feel a familiar force upon you, but...

Morphius rushes to them, grabs them by their collar, and runs out of Egypt. He runs until his legs stop him, traveling almost halfway across the planet. He falls and passes out after being fully drained. Jin grabs him and Silvester. He phases through the ground.

Chapter 13

Morphius runs to the lower axis of the earth, the south pole.

He is fast.

With a speed faster than sound, he travels for two days without needing to take a break. His legs give up at the same time Ares starts his hunt.

Jin is proud of him.

This guy is really fast. And his endurance—next level! The South Pole should be between sixty and seventy thousand kilometers away from Egypt. Impressive! Well, from a son of Zeus, I wouldn't expect less! You have to rest now, my friend.

While Morphius is resting, Jin decides to train his abilities.

That's the least I can do for him. I think you not being alive yet as a kid means this is how my legacy begins, Silvester. We need to defeat him. Otherwise, we are all going to die out here with no one knowing we even existed. Damn it, time travel! Well, at least I know where to start. The only problem is that I'm not sure when it all becomes my present. I have to figure things out. How old will you be at the time I curse you, Silvester? Because that should be the time when the beginning ends and the end begins.

Silvester tells his father that he will be nineteen years old at the time he gets cursed. He shows his father some of the workouts he was known to do in his glorious days. Jin starts working out immediately after hiding Morphius in a safe space for him to rest. His son joins in on the fun.

The first few hours, they run around, trying to find snow to build an igloo, but Silvester tells him to build something less northpol-ish. Jin explains that there is nothing that needs to be bound to a single location. He shows his son the piles of snow he has gathered after running around.

Silvester is not surprised. After all, his father is super fast—much faster than one can imagine.

He agrees to build an igloo with his father. They spend hours building their first igloo.

The first Igloo ever built by us has to be the best one one could ever be able to build. After all, we are gods who will lead people to their freedom, maybe the first to ever attempt to build an igloo. Not many people live here, it seems. Jin says confidently.

Silvester laughs as loud as he can. He says,

Almost a day ago, I had to explain to you how and why you are supposed to be a god, and now you are just saying it like it is nothing new to you.

Both men laugh from their hearts. They are done by midnight, and they agree not to decorate anything. It might give out too much information about the future, not meant for their current present.

The only object that exists in the most beautiful Igloo built for the next two centuries is the bed they end up sharing, and the most beautiful one Morphius alone gets to rest on.

They sleep deeply for the next twelve hours. Though they have superpowers and an endurance greater than a normal man can have, building such an impressive bungalow-based igloo without ever taking a break at super speed is too much for them.

The next day...

Without washing themselves up after waking up, they go outside their home and run around to figure out how fast they can go. Jin sees something beautiful in his son, something godlike. He warns his son, in case what he sees in him isn't something good.

Silvester assumes it is something good. He says, *It should be an awakening. I was aware that something was going on with me after I was able to sense Aries. It seems I am awakening my powers. Running a couple of miles faster than an average human was proof enough that I have powers. And now I am awakening to it. This means I am not going to age and die old like a normal human being would, like I always dreamed of. My only options are either to give up or accept it and move on.Dad, even though we haven't spent that much time together yet, I know for sure that I don't hate you. If being immortal means I will always fight with you, then so be it. I will accept it and move on.*

His father picks up the pace. Silvester gains confidence and tries to catch up to him. He gives his all to achieve one goal:

to be faster than his father, who happens to be faster than the man who ran them through two continents in two days.

Both men are fast—really fast! Silvester is just a quarter of an hour slower than his father at their highest speed. They end up spending their whole day working on their speed. They try something new, using their speed and strength to jump from one location to another, miles away. Jin invents a new skill, the shadow jump, and teaches Silvester the basics.

Shadow jump: This ability is named Jin. While moving at a speed slightly above the speed of sound, one vibrates a hand. The shadow is then pulled towards the user with his aura, and he phases through it. The shadow jump teleports to whoever the user decides to jump with. A sorcerer, whether equivalent, skilled, or stronger than the user, can break the rule of administration if he catches up on the shadow on time. Navigating through a shadow jump isn't easy. Passengers or the user himself can end up in a closed room in which moving fast enough to break through is almost impossible unless one is a natural phaser, which also requires a high amount of endurance, assuming the walls are too thick. This skill requires good physical and psychological strength and can only be practiced by trained speedsters who can use magic. This skill doesn't require the user to be a natural phaser.

Silvester works on shadow jumping and awakens right after mastering it, all in one day's work.

He is still a bit slower than his father, but he is satisfied with his day's achievement. A few hours before their first day ends, they can successfully navigate their shadow jump, where they land, when they activate it, and how long it takes to teleport. They have learned how to teleport with other living creatures and objects without losing too much energy.

Their second day begins with meditation. A ten-hour meditation right after six hours of sleep. They practice to feel the natural energy flowing around them. They breathe air in and out. They feel the dust, vaporized water, and the sound of silence moving around them, all through their imagination. They completely ignore the sound of the wind and the coldness of the snow. They look into each other's eyes, signaling that it is time to level up.

They control their pulse and blood flow, only concentrating on what they want to be. The ground slowly vanishes off their buttocks. Snowflakes hardened and powdered from the cold weather get warmed and melt underneath their bodies. Further snowflakes are attracted to the magnetic field they have created around them.

They close their eyes to focus more on their inner selves. The attracted snowflakes float, creating a hemisphere by moving circularly around and over them in an orbit, letting every single snowflake stay in one orbit without switching, just like planets do around a strong magnetic center like the sun.

Chapter 14

Jin and Silvester are getting better at controlling their energy.

They open their eyes to see the snowflakes flying around.

It's really beautiful, Silvester says. Jin laughs at his sentimental son.

Now, concentrate, Silvester! It's time to level up! Jin and Silvester once again look into each other's eyes without lacking concentration. They move around the snowflakes as fast as they possibly can. So fast, the flakes begin to melt.

Father Jin focuses on maintaining the pressure and temperature in their orbit as Silvester repeats the gestures.

Dad, something feels different. I am burning from the inside. What am I doing wrong?

Silvester pushes harder to reach his father's level. Jin, as smart as he is, realizes the same thing and stops meditating to tell his son, *Dude, you aren't doing anything wrong. You have an element that just doesn't match mine!*

Silvester doesn't understand what his father is trying to tell him. He tilts his head to the left and asks, What do you mean, „not the same element?". The entire training session, we were matching every move, and not to mention, we are of the same blood. What do you mean, "not the same"? Just shush for a second and let me concentrate! I need to push more, moorrree, moooooorrreeee! Very soon, I'll get it.*

Silvester's hands glow red-yellow, and the snowflakes are no longer flakes, nor are they cold as snow. They are now surrounded by water. The water is compressed, and the air temperature rises slowly. The water around them is starting to fade away, turning to vapor.

For a few seconds, there is total silence, and then, *kaboom!* A loud explosion, after which there is no water surrounding them. *Wow, damn, son!* Jin claps and looks at Silvester with a serious yet surprised face.

I was right, though. You really don't belong to my element, which means I have more than one element... Which means I am much different than one could possibly imagine... Which means I am truly a god. Which also means I... am... the... MONKEY-KIIIIING! But one off-subject question, tho, did you also sense a different kind of energy on our way here? I mean, back then, as Morphius ran us to this area? It felt awesomely powerful, but different. With this connection to us, somehow it is different. We need to find out who that energy belongs to. I don't care if it's a person or just a place or a thing!

Silvester breathes in deeply, trying to process everything Jin just said. Everything he said was way too fast to follow.

Silvester holds onto his shoulders and tells him, *next time, just one piece of information or question at a time. And maybe just a tiny bit slower, OK? But I think I know what you were trying to say, and no, I never sensed anything extraordinary; I was hardly concentrating on not puking because of how it would have ruined my face. His running style is weird!*

They quickly change subjects after minutes of having nothing more to add. Jin announces, *Challenge time, baby!!*.

They lay two gigantic stones in the middle of the workout field. They have to meditate and create another magnetic force. Each of the participants will sit on one end while facing both stones. Whoever manages to pull both stones into his magnetic pull wins the challenge.

May the strongest win. Oh, and also, I am only going to use my cold element, so we both have opposite sides. Don't forget to go all out! Add your element to make it hotter! Alright, now what should we call this amazing game? Ball-sucker? Ballsy? Ball-juggle? Sucker? Wait, I have a good one... The planet crusher. Jin winks twice, right after talking.

The challenge has begun; they both glow bright: Jin, blue, and Silvester, red. The aura they ablaze is frightening, enough to oppress a normal person.

Their aura bursts out much stronger than before. Morphius is forced out of his sleep and is frightened for a second. He shivers with goosebumps all over his body. Every single hair on him is pointed in the direction of the magnetic fields Jin and Silvester are creating.

Morphius walks out of the igloo and admires the beautiful work of art. He looks in his body-hairs' direction and sees purple beams a few kilometers away from him.

*This power is so far away yet frightening. It feels like whatever or whoever it is is a mighty being. Brother, is it you?

No, his mighty presence feels different even when he goes all out. Wait, has my brother ever gone all out before? Let me think... I mean, he must be fierce by now. He has made us move along for a very long time. How long was I captured out of this realm? Two suns can not be over right at this moment; otherwise, my existence would have already exited this world. Where are the innocent men I started my journey of hiding with?*

He walks slowly and closer to the beam so as to not waste his energy. Right before he catches up, the beam disappears. Jin is jumping, celebrating his victory against Silvester, who appears to be disgraced and happy all at once.

Silvester is the first to see Morphius standing there, waiting.

Sup brother? Morphius raises an eyebrow and asks Silvester what his saying means.

Jin shakes his head and answers, *It doesn't matter, cuuuuuzzzz, I got the answer to that—ahh damn it! It means, How are you doing? Now stop looking at me like that!*

Morphius nods to Silvester. Jin tells Mophius it is all going to be good, and they will live without having to run and hide for the rest of their lives.

Morphius doesn't believe them and asks how many days have already passed by.

After hearing their answer, he refuses to believe they have a chance of survival. Also, he refuses to go back to sleep and leaves both men to walk back to their igloo.

They sleep through till the next afternoon, right after Morphius takes a meditation break. A new day has started, an hour past noon, but there is no Ares to see.

Morphius at last believes it is all over and hopes that Ares has either forgotten about them or won't find them that easily. They clean themselves and go outside for a walk.

Something is burning.

Everyone smells it and walks towards the smoke.

Jin and Silvester further suppress their already suppressed aura.

Ares is sitting in front of a fire he has just made. Inside that fire are human beings.

So it appears you are all crazy enough to not run away, as I told upon you. Have you already given up on the life Father gave unto you? As for you, brother...

He takes a deep breath.

*...I am very much disappointed! I hoped you would run away and keep running for the rest of your life. I will be truthful with you and tell you that I will not have that much fun killing you. Ok, I just realized it a day ago. I still have to kill you to become stronger and make sure Father is gone forever.You know, brother, without a weapon, my Tomei will be too low to kill an immortal god like him. I hope you will understand and forgive me someday, should there be an afterlife... For gods, I do know there is nothing after death. Odin says there should be something called Valhalla... It is disgraceful talk. As for a half-god, I can't say. You do have a soul. A soul is a form of sacred energy—an entire self-healing energy. It doesn't replenish after death. Maybe it will lead you

somewhere out of this world, not Chaos, I am afraid. Maybe to Uncle Hades.*

After ending his small talk, there is an awkward silence between all four men.

Ares looks into the eyes of each of them and looks a second time at his brother, asking him, *I sensed a very strange, strong power a few hours ago. What was that? Did you get stronger, brother?*

Chapter 15

Ares is trying to find out what caused him to feel strange last night.

He asks his brother why he intended to train instead of running.

Morphius ignores the question and tells his brother that there is no need to pick a fight and kill him. If his desire is to kill him, he should kill him as fast as possible and let his new friends go.

He lays his head on a stone and pleads with his brother to cut his head off, like in a normal execution.

Ares disagrees. He answers, *I already informed you, brother. None of you is ever going to see the next day. These mortal men dared to interfere, and therefore are not worthy of my mercy. Though I would like

to call my powerful self-killing both mercy. Be glad, for your lives are going to be taken by me, the son of Zeus. It is I, Ares, the glorious one who will take you out of this miserable life. Before you have been given mercy, I need to know who you are. Where are you from?*

There is a long, awkward silence; no one is willing to give Ares the answer he is looking for.

He sighs...

And shouts...

He rushes to hold on to his brother's neck, lifting him with just one hand. He begins shedding tears and explains that this is the first time he has ever shed tears for someone, for he has just begun to love the brother every elder of the family hates and wants dead.

Jin shouts at Ares, telling him he should pick a fight with someone his size.

Ares laughs loudly as he tosses Morphius to the side like a bag-pack.

Someone my size, huh? Do you realize I am the strongest one amongst you? Should he die... If he dies, not a single one of you will stand a chance, for I might have fun killing you with just one finger to my sword.

Jin looks into his eyes and frowns. It is the dumbest thing he has ever heard in his life. How can someone hold his sword and swing it with only one finger?

Ares continues, *You are blessed with knowledge. Of course, I am not going to kill you with this sword.* He points to the sword attached to his back. *What I am going to kill you with is a weapon one can only imagine. You shall be the first mortal beings to witness it.*

He points with his index finger up to the sky, back to Jin, and then up one last time. His finger turns dark; it then starts to spark into blue and white. A red-orange flame bursts out of his finger and turns into a pure blue-purple flame.

A flaming sword...

His sword grows to the equivalent of twice his arm's length.

To show off, he walks to the right and slices the rock he threw his brother against.

You see, this is what I meant by „one finger"? It's impressive, isn't it? So which one of you would like to taste the beautiful artwork first?

He leaps towards Jin and shouts, *Well then... I like you! I choose you!*

To avoid losing an arm, Jin jumps to the left and returns to his previous position. Ares' face gets to taste Jin's fist first. It drags him through the snow.

You didn't see that one coming, now did you? Jin gives a devilish smirk.

The edge of Ares' mouth is bleeding. He notices a liquid run down his chin and wipes it off after coughing out the blood that has built up.

You seem tougher than I assumed. Impressive. A mortal has made me bleed for the first time in a long while. It seems you are also gifted with strength.

Silvester and Morphius stand behind Jin, creating an isosceles triangle. They are waiting for Ares to make his next move.

Ares enrages. He pulls out his sword and drags it towards Jin. *I wanted to have some short-lasting fun and return to the golden city. Now* he says with a very high pitch.

He cleanses his throat and tries one more time.

Now I am just angrier, and to be honest, I am going to enjoy killing you, more than I promised myself to be pleased with.

He slowly raises his sword as it starts glowing white, with a light black aura flowing in a spiral form around it. He takes a huge leap and swings his sword. In an instant, he appears behind Morphius, who hasn't yet realized when he disappeared.

Jin, however, follows every movement and pulls a staff with three rings on one end. The other end is blurred with darkness. It flows up to the rings as he swings it.

Ares' chest was severely damaged by the attack.

He screams from the pain.

Don't be a crybaby; barely grazed your body!!

Ares slowly pulls off his hand from the damaged area to check out his wound.

What did you do to me? Ngh!Who are you? How is this possible? Ugghhhhh - I thought the weapon to kill a true god only existed as one whole piece. Other than that, only my sword can be used after the conditions are fulfilled.You shouldn't be able to have it. It is hidden from everyone, and I do not think it looks like this. You have the forbidden tool!!I give you my god's word to never come after your friends. Just go as far away from me as possible!

Jin doesn't care about anything anymore. He is only thinking about finishing Ares.

It is your final breath that you are going to take now. Take as much as you can.

Silvester stretches his arms towards Ares and flexes his palms, making him unable to move an inch on his own.

What is happening? ...Who are you?

Jin walks slowly and holds his staff firmly.

He says in a calm tone, *I am from the future, and I am also going to bury the bad gods myself so human beings can live in peace. Wherever you are going, I know every god will see you before you get there. I hope there is a Walhalla for you to go to...*

He shadow jumps and reappears behind Ares; he whispers into his ears and causes him to shiver.

Tell them there is a new god. I am the monkey king, and this is my staff of freedom. Remember my last words to you and make every one hear of me!!

He drives his staff slowly through his heart.

Ares starts dissolving into golden, silver particles that float away like flowers in an autumn wind. His sword drops off and bounces until it lays low.

And also, I am from the future.. which I already said, damn it! I just destroyed the whole speech thing!!!

Chapter 16

Jin has killed Ares with the help of Silvester.

The hide-and-seek is finally over.

Jin and Silvester discuss how their first fight with a god has been *a piece of cake*, while Morphius is trying to get a hold of himself to believe what he has seen happen.

Am I free now? It feels... different!

Jin and Silvester look at him weirdly and start laughing.

You ARE free now! You just saw it, didn't you? Anyway, what is your plan for now? Like, what are you going to do with your life now that you don't have to be on the run to hide yourself from a hunter? You are a demi-god, you know, and strong. If you want to, you can come with us. We want to see everything the earth has to offer, and as I said, mankind has to be free from gods' bullying. I do have to add that I think the gods, and with gods, I mean Zeus and his siblings, will soon notice Ares' death. We don't have that much time to spend right now.

Jin sighs.

We need to jump now, are you in?

Morphius is confused by the word „jump" and asks Jin what he means by it. Jin promises to explain right after he decides to follow them to whenever they travel.

Alright, men of honor, I think my decision is yet to be made. I shall follow you wherever you are willing to go, for I shall not be able to withstand Zeus' rage

Whenever! Jin corrects.

Jin stretches out his arm and holds on to thin air. He flexes his muscles as he tries to move something invisible to the side. A bright light appears with red, blue, and white sparks around it.

The light takes on the form of a circle.

The heavens roar, and heavy lightning drops down, scattering throughout the land. Jin quickly pulls Silvester and pushes Morphius through the lighting circle, which appears to be a dimension splitting two different locations throughout time—a time-space breach.

Jin shadow-jumps to Ares' sword, picks it up, and rushes to the breach. It closes right behind him.

Seconds after jumping through the breach, Zeus appears…

He is too late!

His eyes glow out of rage…An explosion of radiation burst out of him…It roars, loud enough for anyone within a five-kilometer radius to lose his hearing. A large lightning strike drops from the skies and hits him, teleporting him back home.

Inside the breach

Jin and Silvester are surfing the breach like skateboarders. Morphius, however, isn't happy about what is happening. His stomach roars continuously as he pukes out every meal.

What sorcery is this? How can you not discharge your intestines? Ughhh

Jin laughs and shouts happily, *It is time to jump out! This time we are going to visit Af-Ri-Ca. I think I got the hang of jumping... Ok, now!*

He pulls both men out of the breach.

They fall from the sky, bouncing off tree branches, drifting off the ground, and finally landing in a river.

Damn it, dad! I thought you had this. What the actual hell was that? You missed the ground by a few too many miles. A normal person would have been dead by now! You need to work on that, for real!

Jin laughs and tells them it's all fun and games. Morphius' head is over the river. Everything caught up in his face is still there.

He laughs again for a longer time. Once again, he tries convincing them. He says, *Come ooon guys, it was totally awesome. What are you jibbering all about? I felt amazing! Damn, I want to do this one more time. Can we try doing this again?*

Silvester and Morphius frown as they shake their heads, telling Jin how crazy he is.

No, no more!!

At least no one got hurt, right? The real question is, where and when did they jump? Trees, summer, birds singing, and a river flowing like it has never been frozen before, ever.He did say they were going to land in Africa, but where exactly?

Jin walks around to find out where he has jumped.

Hours later...

He rushes back to both men, still not knowing a thing about their location.

Well, I guess we targeted Africa. I mean, look around you. It doesn't look like the Southpole anymore.

Silvester interrupts and tells him it could also be a country that isn't near the South Pole.

It could be between Continent F and G, or M in summer.

Jin shakes his head. *I don't think so*, he tells Silvester in disbelief. *I have the feeling this is Africa...*

But, dad, you do know that Africa is a continent and not a country. You are good at geography, right?You would know Africa is the ancient Continent C, like the continent in which Egypt is, right?

Silence...

Jin rolls his eyes to the side and answers with a „yes" in a very high pitch.

Just pretend that „yes" was in a very powerfully deep tone.

Once again, he laughs and admits to forgetting about Africa being continent C.

Morphius rubs his chin.

Yo Morphius, do you have something you want to share with us? It's obvious; Morphius has an idea.

Morphius? Are you going to talk or just stand there and keep rubbing your chin?

He still doesn't answer him, almost like he is mentally somewhere other than with Jin.

DUDE!!!!!

He is startled by Jin's shouting. *I'm very sorry; I was thinking about something important. Perhaps my brain has figured out where we are at this exact moment. I have traveled to this area before. It must be on the far west side of the country we escaped from. I still cannot figure it out yet because a lot seems different than what I have explored before.*

Jin's eyes glow with joy, and his pupils take the shape of a white star.

Sooo, about that feeling of a lot of things being different than you already know... Yeah, we just traveled to your future. We should be about ninety to a hundred years from where we just left. Welcome to the future, my friend.

His star-shaped pupils grow larger. *Man! I am soo excited*

He forms two fists and pulls his arms towards his body while he leans his head forward. *We are on the western side of Continent C, the Westside! Oh, man, that's awesome! I haven't visited this site before.*

He switches his expressions fast after jumping like a happy girl for a minute.

He calms down.

*Now, men of honor... Before we continue our journey, we are going to rest for a looong time.*He walks elegantly towards a large shade, plants his staff and new sword into the ground, leans on a tall tree, and sleeps deeply.

Chapter 17

Silvester and Morphius have been exploring the unknown country on the west side of Africa for two weeks now.

Jin is still sleeping in peace.

Weird. How can someone sleep that long? Is it normal tho? Ey yo, Morphius, what do you think?

Not even Morphius can answer Silvester's question.

Perhaps Jin has gotten into some kind of godly sleep.

There are stories about how gods don't reply to mankind because of the long sleep they catch themselves in. Though these are long naps, they are about hundreds and thousands of years long. Of course, people just assume they are sleeping because they all believe that the gods are never going to let them down when they are wide awake.

Silvester kicks Jin every time he walks by; there is no reaction.

Another week has passed; nothing!

After an entire month, Silvester and Mophius give up.

Well, Morphius, it seems like he is not waking up any time soon. Let's just explore whatever there is here until he wakes up.

They leave Jin lying against the tree with his weapons on his right-hand side. They travel around trying to find „the country borders," as Silvester has been talking about.

In this time period, these countries aren't called as they are in the present, making it hard to navigate properly.

They have fun at every single location and take care of the people and their traditions. They spread the name of the Monkey King, making him and them very popular throughout every religious belief.

Half a year has already passed, and Jin is still sleeping. Silvester and Morphius are back. They lay down to rest with their leader.

After an hour...

They sense a strange aura coming near. After a short period, it is much closer to their surroundings, but they still don't see anyone.

It feels like we're being watched; do you feel that, Morphius?

Morphius has also realized something weird about his stare.

Silvester jumps high to the very top of the tallest tree he has found. He looks around and still sees no one, not even from the highest point in the woods.

Weird, so this person or thing—wait, of course! No one said such a strong presence should be from a person, a big person.But there are so many animals and insects here. It is impossible to find out which one has such a strong presence.

Morphius steps up to Jin, just to feel more confident. He wants something to brag about if he can save him from whatever is coming.

Slowly, a spider starts dropping down from its web. It drops to the height of Morphius' eyes and stays there. Swinging slowly from right to left, it builds up enough momentum to jump in Jin's direction. Morphius notices the spider and hits it hard.

Ouch! He holds onto his wrist after hitting the suspicious spider. It falls to the ground and shouts, *young man, you dey injure an innocent spider! Don some heart now! You no go apologize?*

Silvester hears the second voice besides Morphius' and rushes down to find out who it is, just to be shocked by it being a spider.

The spider creature gets bigger. There is an unfamiliar aura flowing, which becomes stronger and more intense.

Jin is pulled out of his sleep. He slowly opens his eyes, shuts them, and opens them once more at a faster rate.

What the hell is going on out here? Can't a young, sleepy man sleep in peace? Just kiddiiiiing. I was awake; I never really fell asleep, I think? He puts a wide smile on his face.

ahhhhhh!!! He screams and continues, *Wait, what the ...? Should a spider be this b-b-biig?* He stretches his arms wide open to show the type of *big* he is talking about.

The spider lets out a little giggle.

Ooohhhhhh, so you're awake, young man. Ya presence now be a powerful one, a no go lai! Who be you?

Jin points a finger towards the spider and says, *Waaaiit a minute. A spider, almost as big as myself, talking, laughing, and not stupid.* He rubs his chin for a while and continues, *I think I may have heard stories about you. You are the trickster, spider, insect, storytelling god, or something like that!*

He pauses for seconds...

You are Anansi! Man, we really are on the west side of Continent C.

He coughs twice.

I mean in West Africa. Is this the country that will later on be called Ghana, the Gold Coast? As far as I know, the Akans must be here somewhere!

The spider transforms into a handsome, young, dark-skinned man with dark, gray hair and, within those, pure white strips within his dreads. He is shocked but laughs loudly, just as Jin always does. His laughter is like a sickness that spreads among the three men, making them burst out in laughter.

Ah you sabi who i am? be honest I lai lai think pesin would find komot who I am, or at least no bi as quick as you guys juss do. Make you juss say sontin wey concern mai tori being told and somewhere dem dey call ghana „later on". U dey say mai pipo are finally going to won themselves a name? you de from di future, aren't you?

Jin, Silvester, and Morphius' eyes widen more. Jin asks the man how he knows about their heritage.

*Wella i am no bi mugu you sabi? I am di trickster god and mai pipo are di akans. Dem no get name for themselves yet.

I juss get reborn no bi too long tey. You fit tok i na born right afta ares kpai. Im locked me away afta I lost di fight, you fit tok I na half dead. Make me tink – technically, I am eleven times eleven years old. Also, I haven't a name yet, I get been thinking wey concern new and perfect name for masef. For mai past life, pipo only dem dey call me di spider-god but I tink I am going to take di name make you juss find me. From dis day onwards I go de sabi as anansi. Yes! anansi di trickster god. Thank you very boku broda. Anansi! supremacy!*

Anansi and Jin understand each other and become best friends—the best of the best. This friendship has the royalty and loyalty a friendship should have.

The four men travel around the world and spread their stories. They defeat gods after gods who stand in their way of finding freedom. They party, they fight, they get stronger, and they sleep a lot throughout the years they keep on jumping into. Centuries after centuries, their stories end with, "They will come back one day and check on us, our dear gods!" Their promise to make everyone free is fulfilled until the last day they are seen together, the day they fight against furious gods who aren't willing to let mankind live freely.

Chapter 18

Many years of jumping into new time periods have passed by.

Jin and his men have traveled throughout time and met gods from various religious tribes. They have eliminated as many gods as possible and gotten stronger. Jin, as wise as he has become, realizes they will never be able to wipe out all the gods at once. He claims the era of the old gods needs to end. Just as he had read from an oracle, which he only had the chance to look into in a „vision" in his dream.

What is the easiest way to make sure they never have contact with mankind again? Even though he has born a lot of children in different periods with goddesses and women, they aren't as powerful enough to help him end this chapter. He has been meditating and thinking for a few months since the last time they jumped, isolating himself from every other person attached to him.

After more years of thinking and meditating, he has found a solution to his issue. He sits with Silvester, Morphius, and Anansi to discuss his plan.

Jin: *So, men, I have been absent for a long time now.*

Anansi: *Oh, ah-ahn? lai lai realized! wella it suppose explain why you de no fun for all, wetin's up?*

Jin: *Ight, first of all, sorry for making our last journey inconvenient.*

Silvester: *Wait, wait, wait, what do you mean, „our last journey?"*

Jin: *Well, actually, I thi...*

Silvester: *Wait a minute. At this exact time, I should be around 19 years old. Wait So it means... No, it can't be! But what happens to this me, the real me, the me, me? Do you lock us away? Wait, do we decide to wipe ourselves out?*

Jin: *Just, shush, ok? That's not what I'm planning to do, although...*

Silvester and Anansi open their eyes wide and ask simultaneously, *although? the heck?*

Jin: *Well, you could say it has something to do with a last suicide mission. But, as I said, I don't plan to put us all to sleep. Soooooo. The thing is, I have the final solution to everything, at least for the time being. I am going to lock the ancient gods away. Also, I have figured out two gateways between them and mankind. And also, they don't seem to have a personally created dimension like we do.*

Silvester: *I think I know exactly what you are talking about. Olympia and...*

Jin: *Yes, exactly! But I need to make sure it is completely destroyed. Olympia just needs to be stripped of its magical, natural power; it should be my first, let's say, suicidal mission. I will go there alone! I need to be undercover and use my brain so they don't sense my presence. In the meantime, you have to find my most powerful children, men and women. They all have to be over twenty-five years old. I need to sacrifice them all. Yes, most of them will die. There is no other way around it, and it will also make the newer generations more powerful if the source of energy gets compressed into a few. I have calculated that there isn't always going to be a supernatural in every generation. This should make them powerful enough. The oracle said there was going to be a maximum amount of one powerful supernatural until it was time. They will split up, and the power will be among many others, both from the family tree and outside. It will be the time when the source is ripe and won't lose energy by being multiplied.*

Anansi: *U dey sure you need to sacrifice all dis men?*

Jin: *Yes, I do, my friend. First, I will cancel out Olympia and then come out from the other side. The gods should be furious, and there will be a war. That's where you all come in. The weaker ones will be some kind of distraction while we banish and kill gods. Sooo? Sounds like a really good plan, right?

Anansi: *Wella then, it does sound laik a gud plan de tin be say. I do need to find up sontin tho.*

Jin: *No!! We just fight together, and that's it!*

Anansi: *No mai fren, I no go participate for dis war. Precisely, no bi physically!*

Jin: *What are you even talking about? Are you saying you want to disappear with the other gods too?*

Anansi: *Hmm...*

Jin: *Come on, man, don't make me do this! You are one of the two men I was hoping to leave behind. Those who will preach while hiding their true identity until it all truly begins. Who knows, maybe I was wrong, or maybe the oracle was wrong, or maybe the oracle is just some bulls. Maybe you could be one of those to make it happen?*

1.

This is where I tell you to stop trying to believe something you should not believe. You see, the last time I went all in, leaving me with almost no juice left, I reached a peak, which should be impossible. It felt like I had almost caught up to your level. I never believed in having such power hidden inside of me. Well, the point is, something happened...

2.

Something I tried to figure out ever since then. You get visions, depending on how high your Tomie is. The first level shows you that there is something called an oracle. The second tells you what the oracle is. You might think, "Well, that is what an oracle actually does." No, no not really! It opens up your vision, it gives you a little more boost, and you finally see what kind of potential might be there. Of course it doesn't show your limit but you still see what difference your next power-up can have. The third one is the most interesting part; it shows you a storyline, what needs to happen, what will happen, when it will happen, and also what might and should not happen. That's where you start seeing the most beautiful and painful part of reality. The fourth level I wasn't able to get the answer yet. I was so close to achieving it, but then I fell all the way back. I tried meditating to get the chance to see everything one more time. I tried exactly one hundred and eighty-six times, just because that was the number I kept seeing. In the last meditation, I was able to get a glimpse into it. He is coming; someone is coming, and he will come unwelcome. I don't know when or how, but I know where, and it will be in the war. Also, I know he is the most powerful among us. We don't stand a chance against him. We will all die! Except one sacrifices himself. One has to give up being on his own, and one needs to be ready to accept him. Only then will there be a slight chance of survival. I have seen the vision you had before, meaning it wasn't a coincidence; it is something fixed, just like your time. You are from a faraway future and have heard of stories about me; many perspectives are what I would actually want everyone to know.

Chapter 19

Sam has invited Lucius, Blu, Emily, John, Jin, Fred, Casandra, and Jason to celebrate this year's Christmas with him and Jane.

Sam, together with Jane, has saved some money and rented a garage in Jane's neighborhood for an entire week. They have decorated the space with Christmas ornaments, two great Christmas trees, massive beanbags, and a large table.

The garage has two floors and a rooftop, which is usually forbidden to use. Because of its large space, they have asked to sign a contract weeks before December to renovate it and make it stable enough for them to use.

The owner, however, has given them an undeniable deal to buy the entire property, including the two buildings in it, the garage, and a two-story building that needs to be completely renovated. Jane, as rich as she is, doesn't hold back and buys it behind Sam's back.

She wants to tell him a day after it is all over.

They now have a large property assigned to their names. After informing her parents about what she has done, they ask her to move out after Easter and decide to cut all ties after that.

They begin their renovation project with the garage's rooftop, on which they place a large dining table at the center and beautiful chairs around it.

They have an entire property now, but at what cost?

Sam, as well as Jane, love cooking and decide to host their first great banquet. They will either share their leftovers with the neighborhood or expand the party.

Creating the dishes and decorating the building takes them three hours, as Blu and Lucius offer to help. The three boys have challenged themselves to work at high speed without destroying anything around them, while Jane trains herself by cooking with her suit on. She doesn't want to lose at the game of speed and cooks at the highest temperature.

All four friends throw themselves to the ground after their mission.

They are completely drained of their energy.

They lay on the floor till noon. They walk home to shower after resting.

The invited friends are informed to invite as many from their known circle as possible. The party will start at sixteen hundred, and they have to make sure to invite more supernatural friends.

Not discriminating or anything; it's just more fun if we can do crazy stuff without having to hold back too much. Normal people won't even be able to eat much; we cooked a lot, trust me!, Sam adds to the message before going back home with Jane.

She keeps a few clothes at his apartment, just in case. Mostly, they hang out at Sam's, as long as there is no heavy-duty experiment.

To be clear... Sam always has two shirts, two pairs of pants, and two pairs of undergarments at Jane's; it makes them even, kinda!

Jane takes a shower after Sam's longer one. They drop themselves onto the large sofa in the living room, watch anime, and talk about their plans for the day.

In just undergarments!

I keep hearing this voice. I don't know if it's in my head or... Somehow I am the only person hearing it?! Maybe it's just my brain narrating. I heard I'm not the only person to have it.

They talk and finish watching two episodes of One Piece.

Watching anime and talking has never been enough for them, so they are playing fighting games on their console. Jane hates losing to Sam as much as Sam hates losing to her. Both candidates are so good that the games take longer to finish than usual. Most rounds end up in a draw because of time management.

One hour before leaving home...

What should we wear? I brought something.

Sam wants to wear something simple, while Jane wants to wear something a little bit more! She has planned this event out nights before cooking. They end up matching each other's looks. Sam dresses as the slim Santa and Jane as a female Santa.

However, a female Santa wouldn't be wearing hot pants and a short top under her Christmas outfit... Well?

She picks up her suit's backpack in case the boys decide to do something fun and crazy, and she needs to keep up with them. Sam grabs her in his arms like a prince would his princess and dashes out of the apartment, off to Eve's party destination.After waiting for an hour, the first guest to arrive is Blu.

Yo, why the hell is no one here yet? And why are you this late?, Sam asks.

Blu explains to him that no one arrives at a party at the announced time. He adds, *That's an old-generation move!* People only arrived on time in the Stone Ages, and therefore Sam and Jane are too old to live with this generation.

The boys laugh passionately. Jane, however, isn't in the mood to laugh after being called an old lady. She knocks both boys on the backs of their heads with the spatula on the dining table.

Ouch, ahaha, they both laugh awkwardly, and Jane finally feels the urge to laugh.

The next guest to arrive is Jason. He is with two beautiful girls and a guy. He isn't happy about being at a Christmas party. He says, *Damn Christmas, total bullshit! You know, if it weren't for Sam, who invited me, I wouldn't even have dreamt about attending a Christmas party. Not to be rude, but what have you even planned on doing today?Let me guess...Sit around and talk about how much fun Christmas is and what everyone as a family can do to make each other happy? And then, what happens next? We just give each other presents without knowing what the other wants, ending with drinking together and then, a few days after that, forgetting the entire set and going back to our miserable lives?All of this gives hope for a day or two, and everything goes back to stupid normal. But, whatever, I'll try to stay happy until it's all over. Now that I'm thinking about it, it does sound extremely rude. Still, thanks for the invite.*

He walks in with the fakest smile.

Sam pulls him back by his belt and asks him, *hey, hey bro. Well, you aren't wrong there, but come on, it can't be that bad? It's just the day when we take a break from everything miserable. But an important question... Why don't you just keep time-traveling to relive the awesome moments? I mean, it's your ability, right? You could just jump back and forth in time, like, every single time, just to witness and re-live everything?*

Jason shakes his head and asks Jane, *What do you think about your dude's idea?* She tells him it isn't that bad, even though, at some point, it might feel like eternity or hell.

Jason shakes his head once more and sighs as loudly as he can. He explains, *You guys, oh man! Ahahahahahah-hhahahahahhahahh aha aa aaww!* He laughs at them while holding his tummy.

A few moments later, he goes back to being serious and continues, *And there I thought my smartest new friends were super smart, enough to know everything. Alright, listen up! That's not how time travel works. You can't just keep jumping to the same event over and over again.It's against the rules, and yes, there are rules. You see, you aren't allowed to distract the timeline. The first trip to an event isn't considered distracting as long as you don't change a fixed point.*

He takes a short break and explains further: *A fixed point is an event that isn't to be „touched." Normally, if you change something you have already seen in the future, time finds a way to balance it. For example, if you save someone who should be dead and the death of this person isn't fixed, or at least not enough time has passed for it to be fixed, time will find a way to kill someone, not randomly, but someone you know. You just don't know for sure who this person will be. Could be a father, mother, best friend, etc. That's one way time balances. It always knows what has happened*

What happens if it's fixed, and how do you know it's fixed? Sam thinks about it.

Jason's face is filled with joy. He loves explaining things he knows. He continues, *Well, fixed is the moment another event is based on. As soon as it becomes past, it is fixed. Some events are bound to happen. It doesn't matter how long you have to see it for it to be fixed. But that's a little more complicated.*

There is silence for a few minutes while he begins to think of an example.

Let's say the third world war. If J. Gades had not sacrificed himself, Continent-C would still be enslaved, and his grandson might not have worked with Jane's father to add the sky cities, skylands to our planet. There wouldn't be twenty-four continents. Well, not exactly! Let's say I talked him out of it, and he didn't sacrifice himself. It would create a whole new world. A world in which Continent-C wouldn't be free, freeeeed?Gades would have been a strict father who might not have let his son take a different path for his grandson to divide continents and add the Skylands. Maybe there wouldn't be Skylands because no one would motivate Jane's dad to find a way to make it habitable.To change something in the timeline, you have to make sure to do research and think about various outcomes.You have to know everything that is built up.As soon as you see something important happen, based on that very event, it is fixed, as I said earlier. It doesn't matter how big or small. It could just be someone tripping over a rock.Mostly, I haunt after events that are forgotten or no one notices, or those that happen a few seconds, or minutes before I jump. For me, it is easy to figure out if it is fixed or not. I have already lived through a mistake once.

He sobs. Everyone knows he is about to say something hurtful about himself. *I once wanted to change an event—my sister's death. She was everything to me—my only friend, my best friend. I went back in time to see for myself how it happened.There, I saw myself. I watched from a further distance.I saw Me standing there, and a second Me at the back, watching from another distance. The closer Me tried to save my sister. Doing so, he killed her. It was always me. I was one of the reasons she died.That Me tried time-warping the sharp object she was about to fall on. It warped back from the top, went through that version of myself, through his right thigh...*

He rolls up his pants to show them a scar and rubs it.

*...and went straight through her heart, right before she would have hit the ground and probably not died. I don't

know for sure.Tears dripped down his eyes right before he warped.The other version of me was just standing there, deciding to do nothing. At once, he disappeared out of the picture, right before the closest version warped.My theory is that how she died was fixed; her death was fixed; the closest version knew what he was doing and shed tears. The other version wanted to do nothing, hoping she would have survived. I'm guessing that somehow, he created another version where my sister wasn't thrown off and survived.He might have created a second warp where my sister fell through and survived—an alternate timeline, erasing him from the main one. A few years later, I time-traveled and knew what to do... I saw my alternate Me and my past Me. That's the first and last time I had and will shed tears ever again.*

So the point is, if you change a fixed point, it doesn't change the fact that it happens anyway. It just creates a new timeline where you get what you want. Eventually, it happens anyway, and you will still feel pain. After you create a new timeline, you don't get to jump back to your original one, and there is no going back to fix the broken piece. The new timeline becomes your main timeline and cuts off your connection to the original one. Every "fixing" might make it worse than whatever has been created.For your entire life, you just live in an illusion and always have to travel back and forth to keep it intact.Traveling more than once to a specific event creates something called time sickness, or at least that's what this guy told me. It leaves a crack in your specified timeline. Either you make a deal with him and break yourself, or you break fixed points, and every time you do it again, you make it worse.It doesn't matter if you change anything or not. Eventually, you mirror yourself or a universe over and over and over again, destroying it completely.

Sam and Jane are stunned and have no words to speak out. Who would have thought so much could go wrong from just looking into the past? Everyone sits on a bean bag downstairs and enjoys the silence.

The rest of the party arrives at twenty-hundred hours.

Right before they start eating, Sam senses something strange...

Guys, something strange, something powerful just fell from the sky; don't ask!

Everyone looks down from the rooftop and notices an unusual light flashing into the neighbors' house.

This can't be anything normal! Jin states.

He, together with the fastest amongst them, Sam, Blu, and Lucius, jump down and rush to the entrance. Jin phases through the door and opens it from the inside to let them in. The other friends arrive just as they enter the house.

There, they see a young man crawling under the Christmas tree.

Lucius pulls him out by his leg and drags him outside. They tie him up with chains, Jin's *ROPES AND CHAINS*. They exit the house and lock the front door exactly as it has been.

The stranger is brought into the garage, where Jason sits and awaits them. He is the only one who never bothered to leave.He looks him in the eyes, exactly like the stranger does.

I think I know you; you seem so familiar!

Jason is confused and replies, *I don't think so... I don't know you, sir! Never seen you before, ever! Who are you?*

The stranger pushes himself backwards and says, *San* with a restrained voice. He takes a deep breath and bursts out of Jin's chains.

Huh, finally! I'm Santa, you fools! Do you know what you have done!?!

He transforms into something beautiful. He transforms into Santa with a silver chain around his neck and notices something exciting.

Hohohohohohoho... haaaaaaaaaa, you are the first person I have met to dress up as the real me! Everyone thinks I'm this fat plump creature! Well, I was. Anyway, nice abs tho! Keep them showing, cuz that's how Santa rocks, yeeaaahhh!!

Sam is shocked.

Are you telling me Santa is actually a slim shady? Hahahahahahahhhhaa, I never would have thought... Look at this, guys. Slim Santa! He wraps his right arm around his shoulders.

He asks him why he disguises himself and sneaks into people's homes, instead of just knocking or passing through the chimney. Santa explains that it is his way of working without being disturbed. He says, *I live in the future and fulfill wishes from the past. I steal every wish made in summer, read them, and decide who gets it and who doesn't. After that, I prepare to go out and place gifts on Christmas Eve. In the old days, I went through the chimneys, but at some point, it was too much dirt for me, so I decided to take a new path and work faster. The modern chimney almost has no room for me. Traveling back and forth in time created a phantom of myself. I only have a specific amount of time to finish my work. If I exceed the time limit, which is midnight, he might haunt and kill me. That's the price. As you can see, I'm alive. Meaning I have never exceeded the limit before.* He nods with confidence.

His body begins to glow. Blu asks him how he can be captured as he is from the future and therefore should have everything planned out. Santa tells him that he isn't stable. Normally, he finishes everything without being interrupted.

Of course I see everything that happens-happened! Something is still different this time. Someone is blocking me. I can't get control of my full ability. Someone here is altering the time flow and making me „blind" somehow. How did you guys notice me?

That would be me! Sam raises his hand. *I have started using my new ability passively. I was able to feel you drop down and get closer. It was something I never felt before, so we had to check it out.*

Father time? He whispers under his breath. He tells him there is something about him that doesn't fit into the picture and that he clashes worlds together. He doesn't think he has ever seen him before. He scratches his scalp.

Whatever that means...

Alright, you have kept me here for too long, and I have the feeling he is about to enter this world. Now, you must help me finish on time! As soon as possible!

Noone responds...

Like right now!!!

Jane gives everyone an ear chip to put inside an ear.

These chips are connected. Everyone can talk and listen to everyone at the same time, but it should silence everyone as soon as Santa starts speaking. He needs to tell us what to do and how to do it before we do! He commands; we act. Fast!

Santa shares his aura so each team can open his time void to pull out gifts. *Take my Tomei and move fast, people!!*

They rush out of the building and work in double teams.

Santa holds back Jason and tells him, *There is a reason why you never received gifts from me. There are many things I have to take note of to give someone his heart's desire. Unfortunately, you were never able to fulfill them. There was always something that made it impossible for you to be noticed by me. I'm sorry! I hope that one day you will understand. Now, go!*

Jason heads out with Blu, Sam with Jane, Lucius with Jin, Emily with Zack, Jake with Hope, Fred with John, and Cassandra with Santa. The other four friends, together with the twenty-five guests, are left behind because they aren't fast enough to help.

Each team works perfectly. They run as fast as needed and generate beautiful lights, making the world look more like Christmas. Exactly at midnight after finishing their job, Santa shouts, *I think we made it right on time, hell yeaaaaaah!!*

Did they, though?

A void opens up right above them. An unusual gigantic creature appears...

Those are hands, and they are tearing up something to get inside reality...

After passing completely through, the strange creature is noticeable. It is another Santa. A darker one with the same outfit as the real one. His suit is darker on the red part and more glowing on his outer white fur.

The real deal appears. How large...

The clouds in the sky are blown away. Optically, the heavens are cut and pushed to the horizon.

An unusual event occurs...

Lightning bolts fly through the cloudless skies, and roaring thunder dominates the sound barrier.

The phantom Santa floats down from above. With a fierce look on his face and his strong presence, every weak soul falls to its knees.

All around the globe...

Not a single animal dares to make a sound or move in his presence. His eyes glow green, changing to yellow. They take on the color blue, fading to red, to purple, and slowly to white, which pierces through the night's darkness.Suddenly, it turns to absolute black, back to green-yellow-black, and back to the original eye color, green shades.

His pupils vanish, and with them is the only proof he has a soul. He is an empty vessel with only one goal: to destroy Santa's existence.

He stays mid-air and looks down on the lower creatures surrounding his prey, who do not bother to go onto their knees.

Without speaking a word, he pulls out his right hand, forms a fist, and pulls it towards his chest.

Warp!

With his dominating, deep voice, he casts a spell. In one instance, he attracts Santa and punches him, making him fly meters away from them.

Lucius is furious. He jumps from his position and grabs Santa, slowing him down so he can land safely.

You good, dude? He asks while looking at the phantom being.

Sam walks towards the phantom. *Who are you? Do you just fight without communicating?*

Santa's phantom floats down to the ground. He is a giant, approximately three and a half times larger than a normal human being. His height is seven meters and two centimeters.

He looks down at Sam and calls out, *Time!*

He looks happy as well as frightened. *Father...*

Time? Everyone asks simultaneously.

Blu asks him once more to be sure. *Are you saying your name is Time?*

He nods. *Time! Master calls Time his name twin.*

Jane suits up.

Her suit has three layers. The first layer is her normal layer. She uses this layer to work out and fight. This time, she has activated the second layer. She knows she doesn't stand a chance in a fight against Time with just the first layer.

She launches a large rock and aims at his head.

Time does something strange. Something they have never seen before.

The massive rock loses its mass and size and falls back to the ground, exactly where Jane picked it up.

What the hell just happened? She asks while Jin warns everyone to protect direct contacts.

Father wants gone! Time must finish work. His time over, rules! He points directly at Santa.

Lucius is fed up with his talking. He doesn't want to listen to a single word Time is saying.

Tell „Father" he should come finish his job himself. If he thinks he is so tough, he should come face me himself, „Father", tch! Stupid!!

His eyes light up red, bloody red. He spins off from the ground and spreads his wings. *Hell de-vilish!*

Lucius punches a wave of flames into Time's sight. After that, he retracts his wings and bounces back on and off the ground, behind Time. He bounces back off in thin air.

In an instant, he reappears in front of Time, right as he turns his head to find out where Lucius has gone.

Shadow storm!

Darkness hides away Time's head. Not the slightest sound is coming from him. Lucius immediately inflames the darkness, turning it flaming orange, and clenches his right fist.

dense!

Time waves around both hands and holds onto his chest. Lucius gives off a devilish smirk and asks, *Aww, are you looking for your head? This move turns everything upside down, or, should I say, it locks away your brain to make it impossible for you to know which part of your body is being moved or where those parts of your body are. Well, I'll give you this: you are powerful, for real! You know exactly which part of your body you are moving, but you still don't know where your head is.*

Lucius falls back to the ground and walks off.

Watch out! Sam screams after calling out Lucius' name.

He accelerates his brain twice as fast as he normally does, and runs to grab Lucius while Blu waits on the other end to catch them both.

Sam, that was... FAST!!. And, you weren't even going full speed now, were you? I was moving at my highest speed and was closer to Lucius, but I couldn't even match up. I barely caught you!I barely followed your movements!

Blu doesn't fully withstand the force behind them falling. All three boys fall into Jin's shadow jump. This changes the direction of their movement.

Instead of falling into the horizon, they fall from the ground upwards.

What the hell are you guys doing here? Stop meddling with my business. Now get off of me! He pushes Sam off of him.

Bingo!

Emily has a plan that includes Jane. She creates an energy ball and shoots it towards Jane, who punches it as hard as she can, while Emily takes advantage of the mess the collision makes, to turn the particles into an illusion. Her illusion is one of a kind. It looks, feels, and smells real. They are in an empty forest with the sweet scent of spring and the horizon... with daytime light.

Everyone charges onto Time. He blocks, warps, and dodges as many attacks as possible. All the boys are in sync and create a new move. Their movements are perfectly coordinated as mirrors of themselves in a perfect circle. They all attack with the same amount of pressure and energy stored up.

Mirror clones of the boys are created for a single second, *universal clash!*

With this attack, they manage to push him back. Right before losing his balance, he steps back forward and blows them away, literally!

Lucius and Blu get up as fast as they can and cut off Time's ears with "Blitz-Attacke".

They haven't mastered this move yet. Blitz-Attacke is a move Grandpa has taught them.

Due to their lack of experience with their new move, they fall to the ground after that, far away from the battlefield.

Time is in pain.

He throws a powerful punch. A punch so powerful, it tears down the skies with it. It is his strongest attack.

Damn it, god mode!

Jin transforms into a gigantic creature. He is almost as tall as Time. Precisely by half a meter.

His muscles enlarge. A spiky crown with golden flakes tightens his forehead, and a golden white halo hovers above his scalp.

The clear heavens are re-filled with clouds, and Emily's illusion cancels out. The hollowed voices and the spring scent disappear completely. Everything is back to normal. Lightning bolts drop from the skies while bigger ones fly from the ground into his crown.

Jin catches Time's punch, and it pushes him to the ground. He jumps back up and summons his staff, swings it three times over his head, and aims at his opponent. Time, however, sees through his attack. He moves a step to the side, blocks the attack with his left forearm, and loses it in the process. He turns with the momentum to pull Jin by his staff and tosses him away with all his might, leaving Jin traveling through a void and falling from the sky.

He falls exactly where he was tossed from.

Lucius walks back into the battlefield with a face filled with anger. He launches from the ground, leveling with Time's head.

Hey, black Santa, up here you son of a... He charges in and punches his right eyeball.

Time isn't happy about it. He has been taking the fight seriously from the beginning but he still isn't able to finish his job. He realizes he needs to surpass his strongest attack and create a new one, and he coats his leg with air and water with his aura as a base unit.

He targets Lucius with his kick. Santa foresees this move and pushes off Lucius.

alright let's do this!!

Sam jumps in front of him and counters with a new skill, *Hollow!!*

The collision of both attacks creates a muted explosion, which teleports them through events and worlds, eventually bringing them back to the battlefield. All everyone hears and thinks is a hurtful high-pitched note sounding through the body like a tinnitus.

Both candidates are blown away, and Time finally falls to the ground.

Santa sees an open moment and rushes in.

Timeless, Silent Night!!

He swings both fists over his head and crushes his phantom in the chest. Everyone is impressed.

There is a brief moment of absolute silence, right before Santa begins to spit out blood. A blade embedded in Time's fist is slowly coursing through Santa's heart. Silent night causes jingles to sound aloud. An angelic tune is heard through the heavens, and Christmas ornaments are gushing out of the attack.

The vocals, the chords, and the instruments are harmonically filling every soul in Santa's range as his phantom slowly fades away from below. The battle is won, but with a huge sacrifice.

Lucius slices through the blade and Time's neck with a single attack, followed by a light air punch towards Santa

Jason slides underneath Santa and holds him tight. He informs Santa that he has finally understood everything—everything that has ever made him doubt himself and Santa.

You are like me!

Santa whispers in Jason's ears, *dumbass, it's the exact opposite! Just make sure you don't gain too much weight.

I too, I... re... rem... remember everything now, and I'm not sorry at all. An... And I don't ask for forgiveness...*

Blood gushes out of his mouth as he says his last words. *Your time has come! I got to choose my destiny, so choose yours, me!*

His eyes slowly close with his last breath...

Sam, together with his friends, bow their heads and thank him for his service.

Jason stands back up and looks at his new friends with tears dripping down his face. He tells them that he has finally understood what it has all been about. He has been ignored by Santa because it is forbidden.

He makes one last decision: he is going to be the next Santa and change things. If possible, create new realities in which everyone gets what he or she deserves. No one should be left out. This time, he is going to search for help so that his past self isn't left behind; he is going to make a deal with the elves.

He casts a spell, *Timeless Saint!* and opens a time void. He hugs and kisses his friends on their cheeks to say goodbye, walks through the void, and closes it behind him. His last words: *don't mess up time. It's a warning!!! Oh, and don't you guys ever think about joining my other version!!*

A minute after the time void closes, green and blue particles fall off Santa's body. His true face is revealed.

So it was always Jason, huh? It was always him! That is why he was never able to meet himself in the past, just like he told us! Sam says.

Jane moves towards him and whispers something she noticed earlier. She says, *Hey, he whispered Master Time as soon as he saw you. What did he mean by that? Have you met him before? Maybe in one of those dreams?*

Sam is confused. He says, *never met him before. Maybe I've yet to meet him. But, as far as I am aware, it shouldn't be possible; I don't have any ability related to time. Weird!*

Right after the particles fall off the corpse, both the original and phantom slowly fade away.

A high-pitched sound fills up the atmosphere...

They hold their heads tightly and scream. Sam, being the only one of them to not feel any pain, opens up Jane's suit to let her out. *Hey, are you alright? Talk to me!*

Jane stares at him bluntly, blood dripping from the edge of her eyes. Her eyeballs are red, and her pupils are dilating to the extent that they take on the size of a needle. She falls on her knees, still looking at Sam, who suddenly gains the ability to listen to her astral consciousness, the soul.

All he hears her inner say is, *help me... My brain is losing something... help...* She drops down to the ground as well as everyone else. Leaving Sam standing alone.

His heart skips a beat and beats the hardest right after, enough to make it visible through his clothes.

His veins inflate, and he hears no other sound than his nerves, the sound they make while sending out electricity, a sound that shouldn't be heard because it doesn't exist. He hears it loud enough to make him go crazy. His hearing evolves to the point where he hears every atom his body has. He hears himself and everyone he has tried merging with.

What is wrong? It feels like my memories are fading away, slowly. But, I can't afford to. He manages to concentrate his aura in his head and heart, causing it to run through his veins like blood, and thinner concentration through his nerves. He sustains himself.

Stop fighting and let it be, Sam!

He struggles for five minutes, with seconds feeling like minutes and minutes like hours. He feels timeless.

Five minutes later...

He has sustained himself and is now doing it continuously without the need to do it actively. His body has adapted to sustenance through superhuman energy, something no other has achieved before.

Sam wakes all his friends and asks them if they feel alright.

Everyone replies with the same question: *How did I get here?*

Jin lays back and asks Sam about whatever has happened.

All I remember is sitting with you guys, about to eat, and then, everything is kinda dark and unclear. But I remember taking on my god-form. Also, my head is still sore from the thorns.Whatever happened, it was madly serious! Sam, you are the only one who is different.You aren't the same as you normally are.Tell me! Tell me why I don't sense anything from you except emptiness.

Sam laughs and tells everyone they've just helped kill and resurrect Santa, and that Jason is Santa.

Who is Jason?

Don't bother, it's alright! He decides to keep the day's event between himself and Jane, though he will tell her when the time is right.

Aaallriiight, let's go finish what we started! Where is his corpse?

Jane suits up and runs along with Sam, followed by their friends. Blu, Fred, and Lucius ride on Blu's and Fred's „deep waves" combination, past Sam and Jane.

Hurry up, suckeeers!, Lucius calls as his voice fades past them. Sam can't let them go away with that. He paces up and carries Jane in both arms, *we've gotta win!!!* They race towards their buffet.

The winner to first ring the dining bell, Sam and Jane.

Miyuuki is sitting at the table, sleeping. Sam wakes her up before the rest of the crew arrives.*Heeeyyyy sleepy head. You are late!*

Jane and Sam stand in front of the table after waking up their friends and give a heartwarming speech. They tell their friends how much they mean to them and what a great change they have brought into their lives. They call their meeting „the midnight dinner".

Emily rings the bell three times, turns on hip-hop Christmas carols from her playlist and creates an illusion of an empty white space. All there is to smell is food.

The friends eat, drink, talk to each other, and dance. Sam grabs Jane's waist and whispers something into her ears. Both laugh and look deeply into each other's eyes.

Kiss! Kiss! Kiss! Kiss! Sam, Jane, Kiss! Kiss! Kiss! Kiss! Everyone is calling out their names.

Sam and Jane smile and move their heads slowly, closer to each other. They give themselves a peck, right before they lock in for a long kiss.

Woah!!!! Yeah!!!! They shout and clap.

Emily looks at Lucius and kisses him on the lips.

They all enjoy the best Christmas dinner ever!

What a day!

On this day, the world witnesses for the first time in history a day that has passed by without anyone knowing what happened. An event that never gets an explanation, ever! Every single person who has slept throughout the crisis wakes up exactly thirteen hours later, not remembering anything from that day.

Sam, before going to bed...

So time knows me? Samuel once said something about me doing stuff without knowing, and I do lose time somehow. But his attacks, though, were fully coated in his time aura and using unbelievably powerful skills. What if I try this?

Emptiness, soundless waves, and darkness everywhere. Jane is frightened and awakes from her sleep.

What is this? Won't you sleep? Is it because of me?

Sam stops his new skill and holds Jane as tightly as possible to comfort her.

Don't worry, I was testing out a theory, and it works. We are going to travel through worlds, and Blu, and Miyuuki... Are going to travel with us.

Complete silence with smiles on their faces.

Sam turns on the night lamp and admires Jane's face

Hey, Jane?

What is it?

Merry Christmas!

Really? Now? Merry Christmas to you too!

Please stay by my side forever! I love you!

She reciprocates his feelings and hugs him tight. Their feelings are mutual.

Will it stay long enough??

They close their eyes and sleep, facing and holding each other on Christmas day.

Chapter 20

Anansi understands everything he has found out through the oracle. His time of living and exploring freely should be over soon, he believes.

He, Silvester, and Jin agree to a plan with the highest success rate.

They split up.

Silvester rushes for the upper part of the planet, while Anansi takes the lower part.

Jin heads towards Olympia and works on hiding his presence. He trusts his plan to not be noticed on this mission. *Should Odin or Zeus notice me... Why am I even thinking about this? They haven't officially banned me from entering the realm!* He calms down.

His new training is about hiding his presence while shadow-jumping. The only problem with his plan is that he has been up there before but never long enough to memorize every part of it. He has only had a glimpse of what the gods' realm looks like; therefore, he needs a good plan to give him time to memorize the most important corners. He needs to get from one side to the other in just a few minutes.

As soon as he arrives at Olympia, he travels through the gateway to the gods' realm.

It is larger than the area of thousands of earths combined. Every god has his own realm. The realm is filled with multiple individuals. The gods reside far from each other, and none can teleport from one side to another without using specific gates.

Jin notices the impossibility of shadow-jumping out of the realm.

Perfect, just as I thought! There is no getting out of here without a gateway. The plan should work just fine. Ok, I don't have that much time to spare—damn, this place is huge! It's like a plate, a flat foundation, just like the stories tell. Ok, I think that side should be it, the second and last gateway home—who is that? He asks.

Jin stops and thinks for a second.

He will notice me and alarm the others. I need to get out of here real quick. No, he has to go! Should I merge with him? No! Merging takes a lot of time. Just kill and hide him!

He shadow-jumps towards a guard assigned to the gates, stabs him with his staff, takes the guard's sword, and absorbs it through his palms. The guard dissolves partially. The reason for this is his nature. Only a god dissolves under Jin's staff. A normal human might just die and leave behind a fleshbag. A guard's purpose is to guard and nothing more. Only his "flesh" has godly properties. His bones remain after the godly side disappears.

He tosses him away as far as he can, stretches the arms apart, and spins around, pulling every power there is in their area as well as the energy powering up the gateway. It seals after a few seconds and disappears.

Time to go!

Jin runs at his fastest towards the last door, and Shadow jumps through it.

The same moment at a different location...

Heimdall from Asgard is standing in front of his gates as a skeleton flies from above, landing at his feet. He looks curiously at it and recognizes a symbol on its skull.

Hmm, a guard from the lower gates to Olympia. This means war. Which god dares to eliminate him? Which one dares to break the agreement? I should have broken the rules and watched over this realm! Odin and Thor need to know!

Back to the last gateway...

Jin hides once more; a different guard is standing in front of the last gate. He thinks about sealing the door from the inside, but it is impossible; the gateway draws power from the physical world down below.

Huhh, so this is how it is. Anansi was right; I need to live on. Somehow I need to awaken my younger self to keep the timeline stable, but that would mean I am going to send Silvester.

His thoughts manifest.

I haven't seen much of his childhood, and to be honest, I don't even know where he is. This is confusing! So, I don't die or disappear while sealing the gateways from the inside, but somehow I won't be able to awaken my younger self by myself and send Silvester to do it. Wait... the time particles of a specific time period aren't supposed to or can't interact with the same ones from a different time period—no, it can't be! It doesn't make sense! The energy is from my current self and will go to myself in the future, which is also my current self, who will travel back in time to make it ripe, so the same particles won't interact from different periods, just a few seconds away from each other. And that version is technically my past.

He holds still and continues his thinking process.

It means I just plant it in a time period to have it back at the exact moment. This way, the time-traveling part doesn't mess with any of it. This could mean I live to see my time again, which also means I have to go back to prison. But how does it all start? What is the true origin of my power? All I see is a cycle with neither a beginning nor an end.

Jin goes on rubbing his chin to help him understand, but not even the iconic chin rub helps him. After a while, he gives up and brings himself to stop losing focus on his main mission.

Right now, the only priority is to get out of here and seal them shut. This one also needs to die! He points to the guard.

I can't just walk past him without being noticed!

Jin calls the guard by a random name to attract his attention. The guard reacts and points his weapon at him.

Jin sighs.

He tells the guard how sorry he is for what is about to happen and confuses him enough for him to lower his Attrak.

The Attrak is an ancient weapon created by scientists of old ages. It is both a sword and a pistol. With enough force while swinging, it can have the properties of a nunchaku. It is fueled by the user's internal and eternal energy. The weaker the user, the less effective it is. It has a memory property. As soon as the weapon claims its next user is weaker than the previous, it will drain out everything the user has, including the soul. For a weaker user to be able to wield this weapon, he has to wait for two years to cool down.

Jin uses this opportunity and rushes towards him. He drives his staff through the chest with a telekinetic push. The guard dies quietly. Jin places his staff on his back in the opposite direction of Ares' sword, his claimed sword, right after absorbing the Attrak. He grabs the guard's remains and tosses them away, coincidentally in the same direction as the first.

Loud horns are heard throughout the realms. Jin knows it is about to get messy and travels through the gateway.

Everyone is preparing in tents. Silvester looks at his dad and asks, *How long were you planning to leave us? We have been waiting and preparing for months!*

Months!? But I was away for just a few moments!

Jin quickly understands the flow of time on Earth in comparison to the gods' realm.

It all depends on the traveler and how familiar he is with traveling through the gateway.

Traveling through a gateway means traveling from spirit to physical and through time and space. Everything about their bond has to be gone through to get from one side to the other.

Not to mention time is slower up there...

I've found out the secret to Zeus' power. As long as the gates are all open, he can teleport throughout. He is connected to everything we have and are. He must be the only god who doesn't need to cross gateways as long as they are opened.

He announces what he has heard on his way back: the gods are going to arrive soon, and they need to prepare. He realizes how much energy he has already used, and even though it is growing back faster than usual, he needs a push.

Anansi pulls him in and merges with him, with Jin being the host and Anansi being the internal boost. The emergence takes half an hour. After that, Jin is more powerful than ever; his heart pounds hard and loudly for a second. He feels something he has never felt before; he sees a glimpse of something covered in darkness and surrounded by light. He is somewhere he is unable to hold on to on his own.

He is pulled back to reality, far away from where he has to be, and remembers what his mission is.

He shadow jumps to the battlefield.

His men are strong enough to hold back the gods.

Silvester feels something different about his father.

It seems you guys have finally made it; you have a much stronger... somehow powerful, but at the same time peaceful presence. You should be able to finish the work, right? It seems like things are going much better than we thought they would. All thanks to Anansi, that old bag!

Jin hears Anansi's voice.

How dare he call me an old bag! Someone wasn't taught the right manners

He laughs and looks serious after a second. He believes he is imagining his friend's voice and mourns.

Alright, first I have to pull out the natural source of energy. He runs around the battlefields and plants smaller versions of his staff in the six corners around them, creating a perfect hexagon. He repeats the same process behind every hexagon until the battlefield is surrounded by thirteen layers of his staff-hexagon.

Jin jumps as high as he can to the center of the field and floats over it. He pulls up his sleeves and raises both arms to attract energy from all the planted staff, a painful act.

The ends of the energy beams are held and connected over his head as he screams out loud. Everyone on the battlefield looks up in the sky and sees his work. He rotates himself with his back facing the ground and holds the knot, pulling as hard as he can until it dissolves along with the energy beam and planted knots.

The gateways have been sealed!, Jin shouts to inform everyone.

He drops from the sky, *Peacemaker!* and destroys the remains of the gateway, leaving a pile of stones arranged in a circle. Stonehenge exists.

Peacemaker: Jin's signature move, which he rarely uses on a daily basis. The name is the exact opposite of what it causes in nature. He named his move Peacemaker because it was used to eliminate a few gods to free their prisoners. The peacemaker is when Jin falls from the sky, holds both hands together above his head, and fills them with all the Tomie energy he has concentrated on his upper body. He compresses the energy. Doing this brightens his pecs, and lightning sparks start gushing out of every edge of his body, making him look like a star unloading electrical energy into the atmosphere. The impact of this blow is strong enough to kill a god if used perfectly.

The gods fighting at the gate realize what is about to happen and retrieve themselves from the battlefield.

The heavens roar while lightning bolts strike down to earth.

Hmm, Zeus was about to make his move, but it is too late. Jin laughs with his men.

The roaring doesn't stop; it gets louder every minute. The clouds change colors from almost nothing to white, to a stormy gray, to black, and eventually red. They fill out the sky. A rainbow-colored circle appears above the men and splits the heavens, erasing every cloud, an abnormal phenomenon.

It rains heavily with high pressure within a ten-meter radius. The pressure is almost equivalent to that of a pressured cleaner. It stops after a minute, and everything becomes quiet; not a single heartbeat can be heard. During this silence, a thin light beam drops from the sky, a few kilometers away from the men.

It grows larger and roars louder than Zeus' lightning ever has.

The fuller-grown beam drops off something powerful.

The high-pressure drop triggers a strong shockwave, which blows away everyone on the field except Jin and Silvester, the only survivors.

What an impact!

Jin is weakened after using himself as a shield to protect Silvester.

Whatever was dropped has completely disappeared. It should be traveling toward the north. You have to follow and capture it, Silvy!

Silvester doesn't move an inch.

No, I can't; someone is coming. Something like a hammer is flying towards...

Jin is hit by a hammer, and behind it is a man.

Thor!?!?! Both Silvester and Jin are surprised. The doors have been shut, with Thor on the wrong side.

Silvester opens up a timed breach and tosses Jin through it.

He ends up in a cottage and sees a young boy.

Silvester! He calls the young boy, tells him what a great man he is going to become, and introduces himself as his father, just before cursing him with his gifts.

He clears his throat.

The day shall come in which my younger presence shall look for help out of a situation. The day shall be in the far future, and I will look much less than I do now. Because of me being nothing, it shall be nearly impossible to find me. I shall be weak and worthless, but a genius. I shall be less wise and not know you. Be patient with me till I begin to trust you. Until the day comes, you shall be cursed with my abilities and live eternally. The day shall come, and you shall tell me these exact words. Remember them!

Giving out so much power weakens him more than ever, and the breach closes after pulling him back in.

Chapter 21

2033

Lucius shouts out Jin's name in the unknown reality.

Suddenly, a red door appears above him. It slowly opens; after that, a second one within it opens; then next, and the next. There are exactly one hundred and eighty-six doors, each with a different combination of colors.

The last door breaks open.

A man covered in blood with a broken arm falls from the last door to the ground.

He is just like me!

Lucius notices something familiar about this man; he walks towards him and tries to help him up.

Why is he carrying a sword and this stick thing on his back? Is he some kind of warrior or something? I heard those types of stories.

The eyes of this stranger gently open.

Where am I? No, when am I? No, no, no, no... what happened? How long have I been gone? Silvester? Where is he?The fight... something happened! Wait, I met young Silvester—that means it is all done, right?

Lucius raises his left eyebrow and asks, *Hey, old, crazy, old, weird man. What the hell are you talking about?

The wounded man starts healing at a fast pace.

Woaah man, how did you heal this fast? Are you some kind of wizard?

The stranger stands up on his feet, fixes his posture, and tells Lucius that he is „some kind of wizard": *Just like you, boy! So you aren't physically here, which means I am not in the real world. How are you able to access my dimension?*

Lucius is speechless.

He asks the man how he knows about him not being "physically" here, *and also, what do you mean by „my dimension"? This place, I created myself, and everything acts on my command!

Jin smiles at Lucius; he asks him when he was born and what time of the year it is.

Well, I was born almost ten years ago, in the year twenty-twenty-three. It is the year twenty-thirty-three, and I will be ten in a few months. Hold on, how the hell do you not know which year it is? Are you a time traveler or something? Just kidding, it doesn't really exist, time travel. He smiles and rubs his forehead.

Jin tells him that the dimension isn't his creation. Lucius is too young to be the creator of the dimension if the man did it ions ago.

Ok, it seems you are young, but somehow still powerful enough that you pulled me out! The way you talk. It doesn't fit your age. I'm not surprised. Kids your age after my time are getting smarter and creepier.

Lucius looks at the man with a straight face and his head tilted to the left.

Hmm, you don't know anything yet. Anyway, for starters, I'm Jin. Well, depending on how someone knows me, I am also called the Monkey King. By this time period, you should have heard stories about me before, or not? hahaha... He crackles at his own joke.

Now I get it! Kid, have you noticed we look awfully similar? Like a mini-me. Perhaps you are one of my descendants; who knows? He shrugs his shoulders and initiates an awkward silence. *

Sooooo, well, thank you very much for pulling me out. Without you, I would have been imprisoned for eternity. I need to continue my journey now, cuzzz there is something important I need to fix. Here, take these!

Jin summons two objects covered in shadow. He explains, *These are very strong weapons. I have the feeling you belong to one of those I have been waiting for. When the time is right and you are strong and powerful enough, you will be able to hold, carry, see, and wield them. Until then, they will stay planted in this soil. You have to work hard. No cheating! I will see you around, buddy.*

He pulls out his right arm.

Wait, old man! You can't just talk so much and leave without me getting an opportunity to talk to you or ask questions.

Jin laughs hysterically. *Little dude, I need to go back to my real time period soon, and as I said, I have to fix something first. If you want to speak to me that badly, you will have to hunt me down. Let's play the game, peekaboo! I will still be alive in your time period. Well, I hope so, haha.Adios amigo muchacho!* He salutes and jumps through a breach he has opened.

Lucius can't believe his eyes. *Did he just say that he was the Monkey King? I just saw the Monkey King! Damn, he is so tall; he should be somewhere over two hundred and ten centimeters. Will I also grow that tall?

He scratches his chin and looks at the sky. *Yep, I will be that tall! That old man didn't even let me speak to him and find out more. „Hunt until you find me," my ass. I will! I will find his tall, old ass, and I will kick it till I get my answers. And what are these things he calls weapons? He could have at least shown me what they looked like. How heavy can they be? He doesn't know these biceps are stronger than those of an average human.*

He tries touching the weapons but is pushed back.

*He really meant it. I'm not even strong enough to touch this stupid thing. Whatever, I want to go home now! Lucius concentrates as hard as he can. The center of his chest glows brighter. Like a chain reaction, it spreads throughout his body until he disappears.

Lucius is back in the real world; his father is still waiting for him, even after his mother has escaped the dimension.

You are finally back! Lucius, you must understand me if I say that training like this is prohibited for you for now!

Lucius nods as a response to his father's words.

Good, at least we share the same opinion.

Lucius stops working on his dimension for exactly two years after this incident.

At the age of eleven, he decides to go outside and play with normal children. A year later, he notices a younger boy.

Something feels different about him; he is weird. Well, mom said weird isn't always bad. I like this one! Should I try talking to him?

He walks toward the strange boy. Before saying hello, the boy smiles at him.

Hi, I'm Blu; you seem nice. Wanna be friends?

Lucius is surprised and looks him in the eyes to tell him what a weirdo he is.

Well, aren't we all somehow weirdos in our own ways? He laughs and holds his tummy while doing so.

Well, you have a point, Sup Blu; I'm Lucius. Sure, we can be friends, but don't think it makes me feel any different about you!

Chapter 22

A short recap of the present timeline: 2037

Lucius' powers are out of control. He is glowing brightly and has something growing out of his back. Everything he sees is moving slowly.

Is everything moving very slowly, or is he thinking and moving at a fast rate?This guy...

A short moment before getting out of control, an abnormal-sized flash of light passes by. For Lucius, it is a normal human movement. He sees a human being in the light; that's what he thinks. The object's attributes resemble those of a human being.

But it shouldn't be possible, right? There shouldn't be more! And this one is kinda special, he thinks.

The stranger looks to the side and discovers Lucius.

It moves towards his direction. Lucius is in a state he cannot free himself from. All that is left to do is freak out and throw out cusses in his mind. He observes.

The strange creature stands in front of Lucius and touches his face.

Amazing! A child, huh!, it says with a fast and shaky voice, Lucius only gets the shaky part; to him, the speed of speech sounds normal.

So there are more like me! He was right! And I almost thought I would be one of the first to ever exist.

The creature isn't standing still; it is moving its legs like one would to count his steps.

Lucius' wings spread faster and pushed the stranger to the ground. Lucius' friends, however, are still stuck in the air after being tossed away. The stranger gets right back up and walks back to Lucius. It says, *All right, I think I know how to help you. You cannot move, now can you? Ok, you can't even talk. Nice! I do have one condition. Don't ever think about looking for me! I will take your silence as a yes. It was nice meeting you.

He walks, runs behind Lucius, and pulls hard on the wings. He pushes them back in with brutal force. That should hurt a lot! He walks back to the front and looks him in the eye. Lucius' eyes close slowly while his pupils dilate.

*Oh man, this dude's eyes are f*cking bright; what the hell?*

The creature holds Lucius' head with his right arm and flexes his lower-arm muscles. Lucius' fingers twitch.

Good, you should be able to move in a few.

He rushes to the other kids, grabs them, and puts them gently on the floor. He runs away immediately.

I can move again. Hey guys, you good? Not that I care or anything. Yo Blu, tell me you saw something! It was this J...

For a second, Blu gives off a frightened look. But calms down quickly.

What happened? One moment, you start glowing like something; the next, we are all laying on the ground except you. Hey, what is wrong?

Lucius is weak.

Hey, are you feeling dizzy or something? Should I call a teacher?

Lucius pushes him away. He tells him to back off because he does not need help from anyone anymore. He loses consciousness and falls to the ground. After an hour, he wakes up and finds himself inside the school's emergency room.

What the hell happened to me? Damn it, Blu! I told you...

You told me what, Lucy? You passed out before finishing your speech, so I took the chance and brought you here by myself; no one was involved. The teacher doesn't know where we are right now. Can you imagine how long you have been absent? At least you know that you passed out. Bro, you scared me there a little... just a little bit! He pinches his thumb on the index finger.

**You have been gone for about an hour. How were you that exhausted? It doesn't make sense! Explain, please! Does it have something to do with us lying on the ground from one second to the next? **

Lucius rolls his eyes to the left side, away from Blu, and tilts his head. He answers, *Yes, it does!* and sighs loudly.

It was something weird and stupid, whatever it is to be called. I hate that woman! Also, you don't need to know, but if you really wa...

Blu interrupts him with a loud and furious *YESSS!*, making Lucious sigh again before continuing.

He tells Blu, *I might be some kind of angel thingy. Somehow, my back started hurting, like there was something popping out of it. Everything around me was moving slowly, and I mean REAL slow. The ball was falling without ever getting to the ground, and your hands were on their way to hit your face, weirdo! My body lit up a little bit, and some kind of—nevermind! Just there was another thing there; it didn't talk, I couldn't talk to it, I couldn't see what it was, but I think I know what it was—everything weird! It came towards me, and then it disappeared. Whatever it was, it put you all to the ground before leaving. It was it!*

Blu is confused, and he asks, *Put us on the ground, huh? Why?"

Lucius punches the bed he is sleeping on and stands up. While slowly walking away, he tells Blu, *You don't have to know! Whatever, you'll just keep asking till I tell you so... A really big wing thingy popped out of my back. I couldn't move, but they were so big I could see them from the front. They came out strong and pushed all of you weaklings away. Let's just say it saved you, because if it hadn't done that, you would have all crashed and been crushed. Now you know everything, happy? Blu starts laughing hesterically and replies, *Yes! But... You said you thought you knew what it was?*

Yes, that criminal, that crazy woman; you know her by the name "_." Though, I'm not very sure myself.

Hmm. Why would a criminal help you and us?

They walk together to class as Lucius keeps talking about his powers and that they are meant for him to rule the world. He claims to be the chosen one. Blu, however, denies his statements and keeps laughing at Lucius' weird theories.

Someone as powerful as Lucius got himself into a situation from which not even he was able to free himself.

This person is very interesting; well done! Maybe I do have to keep an eye on him, no?

I see you

Chapter 23

Eight months ago, 2036

Oh man, I finally figured it out! A way to adapt to every weather condition without getting sick first! Just wear a mask! Like the old days—the old virus-pandemic days! That's the key. Alright, now focus, Sam! You have to finish this school project. You didn't change universities for fun; you've gotta make this seem easy!

Sam, an engineering student who changed facilities a few months ago, needs to figure it all out. He has moved out of his family home to start a life of his own.

Though he hasn't gotten full control yet, dumbass!

Right now he is working on a project he might introduce to his mates. He doesn't know what to call it or what it should look like; all he knows is that it has to fly, *it has to be amaaaaazing, it has to blow minds, and it has to be different! It is harder than I imagined. What do I do now that I have started? Everything would be easier if I had more knowledge or money, or maybe I had some kind of superpower. There, I wouldn't even have the idea of creating something to fulfill my greatest heart desire.*

He sighs continuously for minutes and decides to go outside and meet a girl friend of his.

I hope she doesn't begin to like me less; that would be really hurtful, more than last time's incident. Nahhhh, impossible. She keeps smiling at me almost every time our eyes meet, and last year she gave me a compliment. I am cute! Ahhhhhhhh

He lets out a high-pitched happy acream like a girl and wiggles his toes while leaning back on his chair.

Alright, let's go!

On his way to whom she calls "a girl friend..."

He decides to walk to her and spend almost the whole day hanging out at her place.

We could go swimming or something.

He is truly motivated.

Halfway to her place, the sky starts roaring and turns darker.

Huh? What is this? I didn't hear anything about bad weather today... weird! He runs as fast as he can to make it to his friend before the weather changes. Suddenly he hears a strange, deep, scary voice: *Wake up! Awaken, brother Sam, now!!*

A strong wind blows him away from his path. A barrier of light flashes in his direction; it shrinks in diameter and strikes his forehead. A heavy lightning burns his shirt and footwear off his body. Sam can't withstand the energy and loses consciousness. Dark marks with white, blue outer lines spread from his chest throughout his body and disappear from his feet up to his forehead.

A few hours later, after the sun sets and lets the night in...

Sam wakes up and sees himself wearing only pants.

What just happened?Wait, is it nighttime or is it because of the weather changing? Please tell me I didn't get knocked out and lost time, please?

He looks at his phone to confirm the time.

No, no, no, no, no, no, no... no, no! It is already nine p.m.! That's bad—wow, perfect—and she has also tried contacting me a dozen times! Ow my head!

Out of pain, he squeezes his head.

A concussion, or maybe migraine? Sam loses balance and falls back to the ground. He says to himself, *Maybe I should just rest a little till my head stops aching this much. Too bad I didn't bring a single bottle of water; somehow I'm also hungry. No, I am not weird!*

He is losing his mind!

He sighs as loudly as possible and gets back up just to lean on a tree. He raises his left hand. His bandage isn't there, and his wound is healed.

Am I tripping or something? I broke my hand trying to catch a knife and cut myself in the process; shouldn't it at least be bleeding? How?

He doesn't believe his eyes, and he keeps looking at and touching his healed wound. Such a fast healing ability shouldn't be possible, he thinks.

Maybe I have superpowers or something, hahaha. He laughs hysterically for a short moment and admits it is a stupid idea.

Such a thing doesn't exist; everyone knows this.

Does it?

After a couple of minutes, he can't believe „whatever is going on" and thinks, *Yeah, this doesn't make any sense at all, yepp, yes, I have to be dreaming or something; maybe a hard slap or pinch might do.*

He pinches and slaps himself; he hurts himself, but every time he does, it heals faster than him realizing he is hurt. *Oh yeah, that's a stupid idea. First of all, it hurts less than it should. Also, if I were to be dreaming, the idea of me inflicting pain on myself doesn't automatically drag me out of the dream; it becomes part of it. Thinking about a way to get out makes it a part of the dream. Of course it wouldn't work!* He gives up his desperate attempts to free himself.

This is a dream, right? So how about going home to rest? I can waste as much time as I want. He walks off with a wide smile on his cheeks.

On his way back home, everything becomes brighter than it should be at this time of the day. He shouldn't be able to see every color this clearly. He shuts his eyelids.

Why am I able to see through my eyelids? Why is it so bright? This dream is just getting weirder!

His head aches. Suddenly, he is not able to breathe normally. *Wait, am I even breathing?* A voice further away calls out his name: *Sam, you are awake. You are awakening. Make it happen and come over, Sam!*

The voice repeats itself over and over again, each time deeper than before. Sam recognizes a familiar voice.

His headache isn't getting better. Rather, it gets worse as time passes. He falls to his knees and shouts in agony. He becomes psychologically unstable as he talks jibberish. A stone laying in his path catches his attention. He picks it up and throws it as hard and fast as possible.

And so it happens, the legendary protagonist is born...

Chapter 24

Sam, in pain and not knowing what to do, throws a stone with everything he's got. It glows white and disappears, leaving a white slit in space—a tiny breach. He can't believe what is happening—only the fact that he might be in a weird dream—and decides to walk towards the light. He reaches for the light, forces his middle and ring fingers from both his hands into it, and pulls the slit apart until it is large enough to use his full hands. With the slit torn apart into a rounder shape, he sticks his head through the light.

What the!?!?

He sees a man sitting at his desk and working.

From behind he kinda looks like me!?

The breach pulls him in and drags him to the ground just as he pushes himself through.

It closes in an instant.

Ok, it feels too real to be a dream, or a weird one at this point. Is this some kind of time-travel thing? No, it can't be! He looks like me, but he can't really look like me, like, completely?! This would mean I am in some kind of future because I'm already growing my hair to start some dreads, and this one has it, much longer than a starter locks. This one has his scalp full of it. I just wanted it on top, but not completely. Is he really me? Or is this something like an alternate reality? It was always just my theory!

The man sitting at the desk pushes back his chair and stands up. He speaks with his back facing Sam. *Finally! Finally, you got it, man!*

Ummmm, my voice?

Hey, you might not have recognized it yet, but you keep talking outside your head. He sighs loudly and continues, *You've gotta learn to talk inside this baby here, our weapon!* He points to his head and knocks on his scalp while still facing his desk.

There is an awkward silence before Sam feels the pain he has been feeling before. He screams while pushing in his eyes.

Yoooo. Chill, brother! Stop being nervous; it might make it more painful. Right now, it seems you are fighting against what is within you; it's all about giving in and receiving. Just let go of control and make it flow through your entire body!

Shut up! How, for hell's sake, would you know what is wrong with me? You can never imagine what I'm feeling right now. Arrghh, the pain!!

The man turns around and squats to look less dominant to Sam. He explains, *I might know what you are going through right now. A few of us have been through this before. Our Tomie is special, especially yours! I haven't sensed anything like this before.*

What do you mea...

Quiet! Wow, it did work! We finally managed to awaken your spirit. You should be our number one!

Sam calms down and concentrates. He lets go of every control he has been holding on to. He whispers, *It worked! I feel better now, puhh*

He lays back and looks at the ceiling as he says, *Thank you!*

They enjoy a short moment of absolute silence.

What the hell do you mean by alternate reality? Sam asks.

I never said a word about an alternate reality. It was all your saying, but you are right. It does exist and right now, you are in it.

Sam's eyes widen.

Are you saying that I am not dreaming at all? All-alternate reality!?!?! Wait, who the hell are you? He turns over to look at the stranger's face.

Wow you are for sure handsome! And you do look like me! Are you me? Wait, are you me, or am I you? Who the hell are you

I am, for a fact, you, not the other way around. It's like I said earlier: You are number one, the original!

Sam goes in closer for a better view. *You do look five years older than me!?*

The man starts laughing and reveals his name: *I'm Samuel. Normally, people call me Sam, but in this situation, it will just be confusing. Why do I look exactly like you? Well, that one I don't need to tell you for you to know, and you know exactly why. Don't let my appearance fool you too much, cuz

I am older than I look. Over six hundred years older than you. Precisely six hundred seventy-six years old. I happen to look a bit older than you because my real awakening was at the age of twenty-seven.*

Sam lifts an eyebrow. *Why didn't you just say you are six hundred and fifty years older than me? You are weird!* He sighs and finishes his speech with a disappointed tone. *Just like me... Oh, and what did you mean when you said, "We finally made it"?*

Samuel places his right hand on Sam's shoulder. He tells him, *You see, we are all connected. There are multiple us'. We sense each other and are all born with a strong Tomie; most of us awakened it early in our teenage years; others, like me, had it a lot later...*

Sooo...

Well, you, brother—you are worse than a late bloomer; you never had a spark of Tomie in you.

What you are saying is that out of all the multiple us', I am the worst, non-important version. That sounds just right; as always, I am not important. Even as a me to the world. So I never truly had my own story. A story in which I am the main protagonist. Not even the main character of another person's story. Maybe I should just leave her be. And you still call me the original because...?

Wait hold on! Don't let your hopes down. Plus, I think you have a good chance with her. Don't give up yet. I might be wrong, but I have the feeling the reason why you never had anything is because of some sort of balance, thing, whatever keeping you from becoming you. We always thought you existed, but you never did. It was when you took your first breath out of your mother's womb that we realized you had never existed before. You were born too late because somehow your world...

Sam interrupts and asks Sam to never call it his world, for it is giving him false hope.

Alright, got it! Somehow, your universe thought you already existed. We can't be born as two in a universe. Not until we die or our universe dies or dies with us. We also know that you are a major key character in reality, so we all decided to donate forty percent of our power and life energy to awaken you. Don't worry, we will regenerate eventually. Technically, you have much more power than anyone can imagine, but unfortunately, you can't use it all until you learn to and grow with it. I don't need to give you further explanations; you've gotta find it out yourself. Right now, you need to go back home. Forget about her for today; she even forgot you. If you feel like going for her, do it; if not, then don't; it's pretty much your choice what you choose to do from this very moment.

**So you are saying I am important for some reason? Nice! And why did you change your attitude now? You were all like, "Don't let her go; don't give up!"* He mimics every movement and sound. *And now you are like, "Forget her or choose whatever you want", what is wrong with you? Wait, she is some kind of Mary Jane, isn't she?*

Samuel ignores Sam. He cuts a cross into the air with just two fingers and opens a new breach.

As soon as you cross over, the breach will close itself. You might sometimes hear us trying to reach out to you; all you need to do is open up and talk inside your head. Oh, and before you go, it seems one of us doesn't mean good; he denied sharing his power with you – I don't know if I am right, but I have the feeling you have met him before or will do so real soon. He could have been in your world or is still there, so watch out! You and I will always stay in contact. I have and will always be watching you until you can do the same!

I get it, he threatened you...

He walks backwards and sits on his chair, pretending nothing has ever happened.

Sam travels through the breach and arrives in his bedroom.

Somehow it is trippy that he has everything exactly like me. Has he really been watching over me this entire time, like a guardian angel? Being around him made me feel at ease like I had found a part of me; he is like me!!! OH-MY-GOD!! He is like me!! He is me!! He is the better version of myself, from whom I have everything I am right now at this moment!! I have to find out how he did it; I need to find out how I did it the first time; I need to see him—me—again... Ok, so I took a rock and threw it with everything I had in me... But he did say that I don't have access to everything yet. How powerful can I possibly be?

Samuel's voice speaks to him once again: *very powerful, brother!*

Sam smiles, *So you are there. That means you had to do what you did at the end. I hope I do have some privacy tho, and what the hell is this feeling? Like someone is intensively watching me—whatever, I just have to figure out this alternate-dimensional breach thing.*

Exactly! Now, do your thing!!

He rushes outside his apartment to find a stone, which he tries throwing at his maximum strength. Of course, no breach opens up.

Well that's surprising, not! He laughs hysterically and walks back home.

The stone just flew kilometers away, and this dude didn't even notice a thing! His intelligence is somewhere below. I guess he is interesting in other ways. At least his strength surpasses that of an average human.

Chapter 25

Sam is willing to accept the power he can't use yet. He does not know how to deal with being watched by the unknown.

Did he truly mean it? Maybe it is just him. Now that I can sense things, I know how similar they are to him. Hmm, I guess I just have to train and become more powerful than I am right now. It should help.Right at this moment, what I need is one fat nap! And not a single soul is going to take that away from me!

He jumps into his bed and falls deeply asleep.

The next morning...

Sam yawns

He walks to his kitchen and grabs himself a mug filled to the brim with his favorite cappuccino.

Damn! I needed this coffee. I never want to stop drinking it, ever! I feel almost nothing different about my body. Was it all a dream, or real, like I told myself, „I told myself"!? It sounds absolutely weird, as it actually is! He shrugs his shoulders and walks back to his living room.

Everything becomes quiet as he concentrates on muting his surroundings to build up ideas about his powers. He tries out different poses and signature moves from fictional characters he has read about and seen on TV.

Kaaaameeeehaaaaameeeehaaaa! Bummer! At least I tried. It could have worked like I imagined it. Oh man, where do I even start to figure out what I can really do? How do all those characters know what they are capable of? They make it look easy and effortless. I don't even know where to start. Samuel said something about a Tomei; whatever that thing is...Should I meditate, or do I try drowning myself in my bathtub? Ooohhh wait! Maybe I should try getting struck by lightning like the flash? When is the next storm? Maybe just thunder? Or maybe I just ask Jane to help me?With that big ass garage of hers, she should be able to find a way to simulate a lightning storm-the storm that will change my life after last night's weirdness.

Samuel calls out for Sam. He warns, *Sam, be careful! Hold back as much as you possibly can*

Sam nods and calls back to Samuel, *so it is clear that last night was real and somehow you still want me to achieve my goal, destiny, duty, whatever... but also somehow you want me to not talk to her about it?*

He decides that figuring it out by himself is safer for his own precious life.

Whatever, I don't think I need or deserve this power. After all, it wasn't mine to start with. I have to meet Jane right now; there is no time for useless thoughts. He takes off his clothes and enjoys a long, cold shower.

So refreshing! I love spilling the water all over my head. Though I need to stop wasting water like this, How long have I been in here?

Has he just realized he has been wasting water for the past forty-five minutes? Doubting his intelligence! He was taking a cold shower. How come there is vapor all around his body? Is he boiling hot?No, no, no, no... something is wrong! This shouldn't be happening right now; it's impossible! This is not how it should be! Waaay off...

Hello? Who is out there? What do you mean by waaay off? Off what? Are you talking to me? Am I imagining things?

I am now ninety-nine point nine percent sure that something is wrong here! Did he hear me? I am not even interfering! This is some weird deadpool thing happening. I guess I need to be more careful now. He pissed me off hard enough that I couldn't hold back.This guy... he has earned my interest again! Ok, Sam, continue with whatever you are doing, and don't listen to me; it's an order!

Hmm, I hope Jane isn't mad about me ditching her yesterday, could be really stressful. This time, he drives his car, which he cleans before leaving.

These damned birds, one day imma kill you, just wait!

At Jane's driveway

Saaaammyyyyyyyy! It was about time that you came. How long does it take you to get your ass over here, huh? She punches his left shoulder and hugs him tight. She continues, *I was worried, I had the feeling something veery awful had happened to you! Next time, at least text me soon enough!*

Sam drops his smile and says, *For real, I'm sorry. Something happened...*

An unbearable silence makes the wind around them heard before Jane asks him to continue talking. He refuses Jane's request but promises to tell her after he has figured it out himself.

But could you at least let me get out of the car first before you start punching me, please? I mean, it didn't hurt that much, but still.

He thinks for almost an entire minute and adds, *Didn't you hit me with almost everything you've got?* Jane turns around and spouts. She walks into her house, leans backwards halfway there, and shouts, *Almost everything I got... Don't be too much of a dick about it because I'm a girl! I could be very strong too, you know? There is no need to be sexist!*

Sam bursts out in laughter. *"The girl could be very strong too, you know?"* He says in a sassy tone.

Jane turns around and shouts as loud as she can, *sexist!*

love you too, Jane!

No, you don't!

What is going on between these two? They don't realize it themselves...

hmm...

Jane asks Sam what he has been all about, but he smiles and tells her it is all okay.

We should keep this whole thing to ourselves. I don't need to explain any of this to someone, not yet he murmures to himself. They enter her room for Jane to change into "something more workshop-fitting.". She undresses in her bathroom while Sam awaits her in her bedroom.

Sam looks around in her room like he always does. Today, he notices something different. There is a new safe as large as a cupboard; it looks suspicious. Why is it unlocked? Did she forget to do it before leaving Sam alone in her room?

Chapter 26

A new cupboard safe is standing in the corner of Jane's room. Sam is curious about it.

Should I open it further? Should I close it? What if she gets mad about me opening it? But why would she leave it open if she doesn't want me to see what's inside? Maybe this is a test, but what kind of test? Loyalty? Curiousity? Trust? Does she think she knows me enough? Wait, she knows how curious I can be about many things, which would mean she knows I would want to look inside and find out what it is. Waaaaiiit a minute! She is trying to mess with me! Did she plan on making me go crazy about opening or not opening it? She has this all planned out, huh? Ok, then I decide not to open.

After thirty seconds, he still can't let go of his thoughts.

Damn it! It looks soo suspicious, it's not even a normal cupboard or safe or whatever, she must have built this beauty all by herself. A screen... Sam approaches it and finds a document on the ground, a circuit design.

it looks modern.

Not just modern; her technology is something new, something that doesn't yet exist. Jane is a next level genius!

The main concept of this plan is something I can put together; it has similarities to what already exists. This, however, is totally different on some levels. No wires, her calculations would mean every signal and every bit of energy... electricity should move freely but targeted to its destination, remarkable! Wirelss technology. Can something like this work tho?

Sam is amazed by her work and quickly puts the plan back where it belongs. There, he finds another document—a blueprint for a suit—an assasin's suit.

What is this? It doesn't look like something she would just draw out of boredom; it is something she is working on. Nice combination tho; she would look amazing in this one. It is just like my project!So the new technology she has invented is specifically for this suit! Nice thought; of course, normal technology wouldn't fit inside something like this. It makes much more sense; it should be able to fix my problems. I think her invention would be perfect if she adjusted it to nanotechnology. She needs a little bit of spice. This way, she won't need to fit herself inside the suit. Jane, you are a total smartass. I think I'm starting to like you more and faster than I should. You are somehow a much better version of my existence; you have the talent and knowledge

She places back the design. Out of curiosity, he looks further inside. He encounters an unusual view.

What is this, blood? Jane, what the hell have you been doing? Could it be... that the suit is already in use and you are playing a superhero? Please tell me I'm tripping!

His eyes sweat.

He is shedding tears...

He takes a deep breath and digests what he has found.

The closet's door opens. Sam rushes back and backflips on Jane's bed a little too far, hitting his head against the wall before landing his stunt.

Ouch, what the hell was that? What was that power? What the heeeeeelllll, he shouts.*

The door opens slower than it should—very slowly.

Is she trying to mess with me?

Movements become slower as the door opens. Jane waves around her hair, and that in slow motion...

I am a speedster, just like the flash! This is my power!

He turns his head around. After a brief moment, everything turns back to normal. Jane smiles and tells Sam he doesn't need to look to the side, just because a girl walking out of the closet might be naked.

Even if I were half or completely naked, I wouldn't mind if you stared at me!

Sam replies, "No, I... It's just that's how I was raised, and... never mind!*

Jane turns to her cupboard and sees it open. She murmurs to herself and hopes Sam hasn't looked inside yet. She closes it while asking Sam, *I'm sure you realized something new here—I made it myself. What do you think? It can withstand tons of forces. I am working on a project, and of course it needs to be safe from the eyes of others. You want to know what?* Sam nods twice to signify how curious he is about this new project.

Here comes the truth behind it all. Are you ready, Sammy?

She reopens it and changes her facial expression completely. She opens one circuit blueprint.

I think I have achieved a breakthrough! I have found a way to make energy flow more efficiently than we know now. It can easily fit into smaller spaces and make machines more than seventy percent lighter. Lightweight-free Energy Technology (LET). I left out the free part. Sam, do you know what this means? This is a game-changer! Almost everything should be possible! You were right; fiction can be reality, so technically, there is now fiction. Because there is no wire needed, we can easily regulate the temperature and maybe even find a way to draw energy from a hot source... Sam, Sam are you listening?

Sam awakens from his daydreaming.

I get it, it's pretty awesome, but it could also make people try things, which later on will hurt them—don't you think!?

He raised his voice at her. He never does that to anyone!!

He continues, *I'm sorry! I don't know; for a moment there, I was completely overthinking everything again, as I always do. Of course, I'm happy for your discovery and that it will work, but I'm still afraid it's going to cause you problems. I mean, it's still nice that these problems are going to make you rich after just one month, after the world has found out about them. Just know that no matter what decision you make, I will try my best to support you. I won't leave you hanging helplessly!*

Jane explains to Sam that she understands his point.

I mean, yes, your points are true. I was so focused on working that I didn't even have the time to think about everything that could go wrong. Even if your point wasn't accurate, I would still make sure you don't just speak empty words; after all, the whole theory of it being possible and how it could work was your thinking; I just took it and added my spice to it, like with the resources and the missing calculations. You are an important part of what I do. The most important part is that we do the theory part; I organize and build, and you do the future overthinking thing. Sometimes it gets on my nerves, but you are always right. This makes us the perfect team; we fit perfectly!

How did this whole situation turn around into some kind of... this!?!

Chapter 27

Sam, the last time you wanted to come visit me, I waited for you, and you never came. Jane asks.

I'm sorry, something came up, and I have told you this several times. I'm sorry! I'm here now; this counts too, right? Sam gives a sincere apology. With his shaky voice, Jane can feel how much it means to him and doesn't ask further questions.

Maybe it was an emergency, like something serious... She thinks. *... first of all, this needs to stay closed until the time is right. He doesn't need to know about it yet.* She closes the safe and locks it.

Sam accepts the fact that he isn't going to get any explanations about her suit. He does not want to start an argument and leans back on the bed, holding up his body by placing both hands behind his buttocks.

Jane bites the edge of her lower lip. *The way you are sitting and staring at me right now—are you flirting with me? Not that it matters, tho...* She rolls her eyes to the side.

You wish, what if I did? He teases her, and makes her blush.

She coughs out of embarrassment. She pushes up her cheeks and chooses to change the subject; *Soooo, what is so urgent?*

Sam laughs. He lays back further and stares at the high ceiling. *It's just... I was thinking about „super powers," you know?* He shrugs his shoulders and waves both hands around, randomly.

Jane smiles. She turns away for a few minutes and turns back around with a serious face.

She doesn't think he's crazy; she knows something!

She walks towards Sam and places her hands on his shoulders to pull him towards her.

Super powers? You believe in them, too? I always thought that you were joking around, but you really do believe in them, don't you? Why haven't you ever told me about your passion for them? Your eyes are glowing. This is true passion!

Sam scratches his scalp and tells her that he has been telling her about superpowers ever since the day they met.

Calm down, Jane! You've already heard it several times.

Yeah, well, that doesn't mean you believed in them, tho. I could also be talking about the Greek gods and stuff, but that doesn't mean I believe in them. Okay, that's a bad example because they don't exist, and that's a fact!

Sam doesn't agree with her statement.

Why should superpowers exist but not gods or Greek gods? Do you also not believe that God exists?

With her female intuition, she senses negative emotions from Sam.

Ok, just hear me out, OK? I never believed in superpowers. As you know, for me, the only superpower in existence for humanity was technology. Technology should have been the only great superpower to exist. The only thing missing in the equation and in the statement was the "invisible" connection from one medium to the other. That was the only thing that motivated me enough to work on your idea, well, theory, and I achieved the goal. I did everything... perfectly. I said to myself, „Sam is going to be really proud of me. He might look weirdly when I show him my superpower. He might even be able to blush through his dark skin." It made me happy, and it seems like it was the first step for me to see reality. For the first time in my life, I saw something unexplanable. I saw someone do the impossible. It was a young boy; he was playing with a flame, Sam, a flame that came out of his bare hand and shot it against his friend, who didn't even seem to be bothered about it. He just slapped it out of the way, also with his bare hand! It wasn't the only weird thing I have seen so far; there are much more out there, good and bad. She frowns and looks steadily over Sam's head. She is serious about what she is saying. *What if there is no one out there who could stop the bad ones? Someone has to do something!*

Sam knows what she is trying to say. He knows that she wants to be a hero and that she has already started it. He is worried about her and pulls her to lay beside him. He places his palms on the back of his head and lays on them.

Stop it, Jane! It's enough! I have the feeling that you are talking about heroism. Imagine a world full of heroes and villains. You have seen the movies and series, right? You now know you were wrong, and there are many new things out there that might or might not be beyond your understanding. Of course, it might have been the first step into seeing what reality is, and I don't doubt you; I believe you are telling the truth. You are telling me it is some kind of step into figuring out new steps; you are smart enough to put things together and finally admit that there are such forces as gods and God with the capital "G." I don't think we need to be arguing about this fact. You have found out what they are capable of. I want to tell you not to even think about dealing with them, but somehow, I have the feeling that you want to play a hero. Just stop! Cancel that thought! There isn't going to be anything hero-ing for you. You are going to get yourself hurt, and I don't like the thought of it, so just don't, ok? Please!

What tension! You could cut it with a knife...

Jane is totally quiet; she doesn't say a word. She understands Sam's feelings, he cares for her.

I'm sorry for pushing myself in too deep, he says. *I was hoping you would help me try out different things, like from the comics, sci-fi, and stuff where most of them have accidents to trigger their powers. I thought it would be "fun," relatively. I get it if you don't want to do it.*

Jane shushes him and agrees to help him out. She asks him to follow her to her workshop, and she shows him something amazing.

I had these dreams where I built something like this but never found out what I had to do with it. It was always just a plan, and I built everything I saw. Never tested it out before, and I don't know what it does. But assuming you somehow, for some reason, do have some kind of superpower, this might be the key to finding it out. It's just a theory, I don't know. Wanna try?

Sam nods.

What do I do?

Jane opens up the machine. Inside is a chamber in which only a person can lay down. She remembers all the controls she has seen in her dreams. She pushes every button, pulls every lever there is, and closes the chamber. She then connects with her personal AI assistant.

Ok, Sam, it is ready. Are you ready for some fun? Sam shouts, *Yes! But will it hurt?*

Jane answers with *no* and then *yes*, followed by *maybe*.

She has yet to find out how the machine is going to work.

She whispers, *with or without a change, I hope you don't die or become cocky—I love you, and I hope one day you will see it and do the same too.*

She pushes the last button on her computer after entering the command station and locking the doors.

Chapter 28

Whamm, Kabooom

Silence...

The entire workshop has been shaken down by the experiment. This happened...

The machine was online for the first few minutes, and it worked perfectly. It disconnected itself from the AI and server and started to work on its own without Jane interfering. Suddenly, it started sucking up all the air the room had. It was fully sealed; not even air could enter the chamber. The suction continued until there was no air left inside; the room turned into a huge vacuum space. Jane tried everything she could to open up the door, or at least the vents, but nothing was possible by that time. Sam was put into deep sleep since the machine was online. The vacuum state was sustained for ten minutes. With Sam as the only exception, everything in the room was deeply frozen. The temperature dropped down quickly and stayed that way until...

The machine started vibrating. It was sure that the temperature hadn't reached absolute zero yet. The chamber began to glow, the sucked air was slowly released back into the room, the temperature began to rise until it reached exactly twenty-one degrees Celcius, and then...

Silence... Still silent. All one could have heard was Jane's heart beating really fast while Sam's was beating abnormally fast. It was impossible to detect a heart rate; his heart beat around three hundred and sixty-five times per second. And there was a high-pitched tone inside the ear—unbearable. It should have been impossible for a normal human to hear. A shock wave was released from the machine; it crashed down on everything inside the room. Even itself and the strongest glass in the world standing between Jane and the room weren't left unharmed. The glass was cracked with an opening on each corner, and the shockwave tossed Jane away, crashing her against the wall behind her.

After being unconscious for half an hour, she gets up and looks for Sam.

How did she...

The machine she created is to be one-use-only. It is built to be used once and then lose all its functionalities.

Sam! Sam, are you there? Are you alright? Where are you? Just say something—just a sound, please!

Jane is devastated. Though she has taken precautions and stayed further away from the machine behind the strongest glass she has had at home, she is partly affected.

But what happened to her though?

Jane is still looking for Sam. The room and the chamber are empty, but Jane discovers something... A hole has been created through the machine to the ground beneath it.

The internal part of the machine was blown into the ground. So the part of it in which Sam was sitting is now buried underground? What have I done? Did I just kill Sam? I'm very sorry; I didn't mean to! Dear God, please, if you exist, then show me a wonder! Show me it and let me find him, at least on the edge of death. I don't want him to go, please! Just this one time, show me there is a higher power out of my reach, my reasoning, my understanding, please!

The room is quiet.

Maybe "God" doesn't give a damn about her—or maybe there really isn't a „God" or a „higher power" out there, just as she thought. How does it feel to hope you were always right in a situation where you wish you were wrong? People deny faith but then hope for it when it suits them the most—ungrateful! Is she crying? This is the first time she has ever cried for someone or anything in general! Jane, this time it is really going to hurt; even I have lost one of the most interesting people. You do deser...

cough, cough, cough! Someone is in there!

Since when do you believe in a higher power? An echoed, shaky voice sounds from beneath. *Is this your redemption, Jane?It is Sam. He asks Jane why she thinks that he is dead. Jane can't believe her ears. She hears a familiar voice and pushes aside the broken pieces of the machine to jump through the hole without thinking twice.

Sam! She cries out. Her voice echoes throughout the room. *Sam, thank you very much; you're not gone yet!* She finds Sam and hugs him as tight as she can.

Wait, "gone yet"? Wooow, thanks!

Sam has never seen her in this state before; he experiences a beautiful feeling, being wanted. For the first time in his life, he feels the warmth of being wanted and needed by someone.

One can tell that a very heavy weight has been lifted off Jane's shoulders. Sam enjoys the moment and hugs her tight.

Jane, were you crying? So you can cry? I am really the bad boy; I even got you crying. Would you look at that!?

Jane buries her face on his neck and takes a bite. *Shut up, j*rk! Never leave me like this again!* They take a moment for themselves. They realize that the hole isn't just a normal hole. The explosion has created a new room. Or was it always there, just that no one ever knew? The floor is like a sanctuary; the walls have drawings and ancient writings on them. They are telling one whole story about a traveler finding himself, and that from different perspectives. They name him the preserved rebel. Sam recognizes a part of the writing; it was written on Samuel's bedroom wall. And the meaning: "The last two of them would have to unite as light and darkness in one. The hated twins will know about one and only one, for it is one who belongs... They are the last ones to take over."

He thinks to himself, *We need to have more in common than having the same face.*

The center of the room is clean and has more writing on the ground. It says, „You are the first to see this. Look for the missing chapters and end the story while being your whole self!" It disappears after Sam reads it out loud.

*What does it mean?***Jane, I don't know. I'm also seeing this for the very first time!**

Jane promises to decrypt the writings. Sam promises to help find out what they mean. They walk upstairs into Jane's room.

Wait a second, something happened to you! What are these tattoos all over your body? You don't do tattoos, and how the hell are you able to walk normally after everything that happened?, Sam?!

Chapter 29

Sam's body is fine after the explosion. His body doesn't have any signs of scars or wounds.

Jane has seen the last scar heal, leaving no trace of blood on his skin. Though his pants are fully coated with his blood, As for his shirt, it is no more. It didn't make it out whole.

Jane asks Sam about his experience. Also, she is curious about how he is doing. Sam stares at her and notices her skull bleeding.

What happened to you? Are you alright?

Jane figures that Sam is trying to change the subject. She insists, *I am not answering before you give me an answer!*.

What are you going to do now Sam? Tell her the truth or lie? Samuel asks.

Sam takes a moment for himself. His brain is working faster than a normal brain should. His thinking process is accelerating fast; everything he sees is moving slowly, just like before. This time, he is doing it deliberately.

What do I tell her now? I could come up with a super nice story that actually might make sense-no, she doesn't deserve that! I think her wound came from whatever that was that happened. But also, she's keeping a secret from me! In her suit, it looks like she has been doing this for a very long time now. Should I ask her about that? No, I shouldn't. It just feels wrong! I will find another opportunity to ask her about it; I hope it isn't too late then.

He slowly decelerates his thinking and decides not to lie to Jane.

Alright then, listen. Yes, as it seems, the experiment worked. I have a hunch about what I am capable of, but before I understand myself, I won't be able to give you an accurate answer. I just know I am more than fast enough now. I still need to find out how to handle all... this. He waves his hands around in the air and points them to the ground. Jane, even though she doesn't like the idea of him not telling her anything, tries to understand his situation and tells him that she is going to wait until he is ready. They cook and have a meal, after which Sam says goodbye and heads back home.

Three weeks later...

Sam is outside training to control his speed. It is hard for him to move at an abnormally fast pace and accelerate his thinking process. His speed doesn't require normal body movements; there are still a few steps attached to it, he thinks.

Alright, I can now hold it up for like forty seconds. I don't feel tired, but I still can't hold it upright. The farthest I have gone so far is about fourteen kilometers. It's not really that bad, but somehow I always get thrown... dragged away. Nature doesn't seem to like me that much, now does it? I need to figure out a way to keep it up. I might even be able to go faster and farther if I get it under control. He sits on a tree stem.

Ok, let's try something different

This morning, something beautiful happened. Sam was able to let out some of his energy-a spherical shape full of his energy. He saw, heard, and felt almost everything within the sphere.

What if I focus on this sphere first? I think I am not the only one gifted. Because it actually exists, there might be others like me there, and I have to make sure to let out as little energy as possible. Something like suppressing my aura or so. It should be at a minimum so that even I will have difficulties sensing it. K, let's do this!

He focuses every ounce of his brain cells on creating the perfect cell. He starts with a sphere to cover a one-kilometer diameter.

Alright it is working. Now it has to be much thinner.

He stands upright and stretches both arms to the side. He motivates himself. *Concentrate! Thinner!*

He enlarges the sphere while keeping the energy output stable.

After a few seconds, his hard work bears fruit; he is not losing too much energy. Though it is the perfect amount and perfect skill, he discovers an issue: the positive and negative abilities of his skill: He sees, hears, smells, and feels everything-an overwhelming ability. Everything is blurred and contains unuseful information. He forgets himself in the process.

*Damn it! What the hell!? Everything is so... ughhh! Sh*t! This sh*t hurts! Ok, concentrate, dude... Concentrate! You need to tell everything apart. I need to focus on important, interesting, and fantastic information. My three-d printer is still on. Maybe find my way there and watch it work? Alright, my apartment lies in this direction, My room should be up there. Wait, restart! I have to do everything with brain acceleration. Next try! Alright, now, pretty fast home, and then up, up, up, and there we go. Now entering... perfect! Three-d printer is right here and working fine.*

He has achieved something new. An ability perfect for spies. He makes its base-ability and works on precision. Focusing on new targets at the same time is his next goal.

Now, focus on something different, don't lose your current target.

He speeds his thoughts to find an interesting target and expands his sphere to cover the entire planet, its orbit, and even the sky-lands. He names his passive ability "God's seventh sense."

God's seventh sense: invented by Sam. The name "seventh sense" comes from "sixth sense." The seventh sense is the ability to use all six senses freely without limitations. The body's functionalities become sensitive; even the touch of a target from kilometers and miles away can be felt. The main source of this ability is the user's consciousness. He has to know and believe in what he is capable of and eliminate the limits to his understanding. It strengthens the user, depending on which race of aura he belongs to. The ability transforms the user into a god, but Sam has yet to figure out the possibilities. The user of the ability has to be skilled to use it properly. A less skilled user moves around with his sphere and becomes the center of the source. Sam, however, is skilled. He has inveted the skill through which he is not the center of source. Should he be moving around, the sphere will never follow him. He will be a game player and move around in his own field, he will be able to move throughout his sphere, as long as he doesn't decide to relocate or deactivate it.

What about Jane? She isn't home! What about her scent-none? Her voice? There it is, very weak. A clooser look He sighs as loud as he can. *The suit-she is inside it! She really is using it. She is a bad-ass though*, he whistles

Jane has stopped fighting. She is frozen and being beaten up. Her tummy is being kicked in, and her head is stomped on. Sam sees her losing and runs to her as fast as he can. Missing her by a few meters, he goes: *thirty seconds of stability, stopping is still a problem, tho - Hey, are you ok?* He walks towards her and pushes the guy to the ground.

How did this dude get here? Did he just toss me with one arm? He didn't show any signs of struggle! The stranger is tall and bulky. He is surprised by what Sam has done. With a voice filled with anger, he asks, *Hey you! Are you also looking for a fight?*

Wow, his ego seems to be the only thing bigger than his forehead, Sam thinks after seeing him.

He breathes out heavily and clenches his fists. He turns and tilts his head to look at his enemy with the fiercest glance his face can show. The guy is frightened and walks backwards, slowly. He takes off his shoes and runs as fast as he can. Sam carries Jane in his arms and runs back to his training field. Her mask, which appears to be a helmet, opens up for her to puke out everything built up from Sam's messy run.

Where am I? What happened? She flinches and asks, *Who are you?*.

Umm, you good, Jane? Sam asks as he wipes off the remaining puke on the edge of her lips. Jane opens her eyes wide, shuts them close, shakes her head, and opens them again.

Oh Sam, it's you-um, I mean, sir, you seem like a very nice person. Thank you!

Sam's stares with a serious face; *Jane I know it's you, and besides, you don't even have your helmet on anymore! I figured out what you have been doing! Was it something you were ever going to tell me?*

Jane looks away. She is too embarrassed to look into his eyes. She feels Sam's disappointment. She keeps her eyes focused on the ground and sits up.

Since when do you know? How did you find out?

Sam tells her that he has known about her secret for a while now. He has seen a woman in a suit jump from one roof to the other.

Moments ago, I was working on an ability, and then I saw what exactly you do with your suit

She pulls back, raises her head, and wipes off her tears. She pleads, *Listen, I'm sorry you had to find out this way. To be honest, I didn't know if I should tell you or not; actually, I was afraid of how you would react once I told you. But why haven't you said anything about it until now? Were you just waiting for the moment where you would just rub it in my face? Why?*

She sniffs everything that's trying to come out of her nose. She is crying not only because she is feeling guilty but also from the pain after she got beaten, and Sam's running is a major criteria.

Jane, why would I want to do that? You should know me well enough to know that I wouldn't do such a thing, and more importantly, not to you! I was waiting for the moment when you would be ready to trust me on this one. Are you hurt? He beat you up, baaaad!

Chapter 30

Jane sighs. She looks to her left, then to her right. She sighs once more and rolls her eyes up and down.

Is something wrong with her? Is she really hurt? Sam thinks. He wants to know if something has happened to her and asks again, *Jane, are you hurt?* She pulls her legs towards her chest and holds them tight. *You don't look okay, Jane! What happened?* Jane looks up and stares at the ceiling. She stretches out her legs and falls back to lay on the ground. She tells Sam, *Hey, can you lay down beside me?* She places her hands on her tummy.

Sam, without hesitation, slides off the log to the ground, facing her. Jane smiles for a brief moment and asks Sam, *What do you think happened? Did you see or hear anything? Were you there the entire time?*

Sam takes inhales deeply, exales, and sighs. He copies her and lays back with his feet facing Jane's. He places his hands on his tummy.

I saw almost everything. From the moment you were fighting like a badass to where they started kicking and punching, leaving you with nothing to do to defend yourself, it was like you were blacked out or something. I wasn't really there, though

What do you mean, you saw everything but weren't there?

Sam answers, *japp, japp. It's exactly as I said*

Jane is a bit surprised. She has imagined something extraordinary happening, but not what Sam is talking to her about. Her surprised look quickly changed into a trusted one. With finger signs, she fully opens up her suit and takes it off. She sits upright, facing Sam. She places her head on her right knee.

Tell me more about... everything! She pulls his legs and spins Sam around before stretching out her legs to place Sam's head on them. She strokes through his dreads.

You see... He pauses to think and continues. *My power lies in speed, it seems, but somehow, I think there is more to it. It feels like something that doesn't belong to me, like some kind of greater power. I haven't figured it out yet. But it feels like I have large reserves. I might need to find out where my max is and what I'm capable of doing. I only know that right now, there is almost nothing I can't do. My only issue is control. I can't control my abilities well; sustaining my energy is hard. I can run fast, like reeaally fast. The problem is that I can't run for long and am trying to stop. I can't run like I did before; there is no normal running for me anymore. Do you wanna know what it feels like to run?*

Sure! Jane answers. Her curiousity is at its peak.

*Ight! It feels like something keeps pushing and pulling on me. It could be air, or maybe the god of nature, or space;

I don't know. Imagine a plane flying through a storm, or the storm deliberately hitting from the side and moving the flaps. That's what it feels like. Can you imagine? For a distance, you are pulled back and forth; for the next, you are flying and pulled to the left and right, and up and down. Consistently reacting. *Stopping is also not easy to do. My timing is always wrong. I miss the chance to move slower bit by bit and end up flying for real*

Jane stops stroking his hair for a second and adds, *Maybe I can help with that. But what about the seeing stuff? Does it have something to do with running? Because you are bending light and time at your speed?*

Sam starts laughing and says, *I wish! Unfortunately, I ain't that fast. Maybe a little. Before running, I just imagine everything being very far away from me, like decreasing the size of my pupils. Like bending space, light looks bent. Space is curved, and the distance feels greater. It helps me a bit. It's this focussing kind of thing. I was working on retracting my pupils and found out I have a talent for it, so I came up with a theory; "What if space is bent in my sight and everything seems farther than it is in reality? I focused on it and added the pupil-retractions. I figured I could let loose an amount of energy and perceive more. This gave me the idea of trying to use it another way. I focused on letting a small amount of energy into the atmosphere. Small enough that I could regenerate faster than I use it, though it doesn't matter because I have more than enough of it. I spread it out to make it thin, thinner than air, more like light—so there is no pressure or weight with it. It can't be seen or felt. Well, it worked on the first try. It just hurt pretty bad the first time. I could sense, see, smell, and taste everything there was, even the sky. I am one of the first human beings to see them. I asked myself again, „What if I just focus on a few things in the meantime until I get used to it?" I tried finding things in my apartment and looking through the building to see what my neighbors were doing. That was one big mistake!!* He scratches his scalp and laughs awkwardly.

Jane laughs with him. *Let me guess, you saw a few naked moments you really didn't mean to see?* Sam raises both thumbs and whispers, *yupp*.

He continues, *Anyway, I wanted to see you because we haven't talked for a long while, so I looked through your home, garage, and workshop, but you weren't there. I intensively focused every ounce of concentration I had on you, and then suddenly, you were there, but in your suit. I watched the entire fight and admired your moves.. until, yeah, you know what... happened. What was wrong?* She tells Sam not to laugh after hearing what has happened out there. Sha says, *It is an energy problem. Then Suit ran out of energy. It freezes as soon as the battery is low. The reserved energy is to keep it unharmed from the outside. I have tried to find a solution, but until then, I have to live with this issue. The suit was finished about three months ago, so apparently it isn't enough time to come up with something stable.* Sam tilts his head to the left, turns around to look at her, and asks, *Now why the hell would I want to laugh about it?*

Jane is embarrassed.

Well, someone like me shouldn't have a problem finding a solution. I am terrible; I am useless! Look at my dad! He figured out a way to use the rings around our planet. At the same age as I am right now. Look how hard they are working under his leadership to create new islands. And what have I done until now? All I have done is build little machines for you, the suit, and this massive machine that exploded or imploded, I dunno, after the first run. It is not enough, Sam! I am useless! She begins to cry.

Sam holds her hand and strokes it with his fingers. He calms her down by telling her, *You aren't useless, Jane! You are amazing! Just look at your suit; it was made by discovering a new type of technology. Right now, you are preparing for a patent, which means your dad was never able to achieve this level. Sure, of course he discovered there is atmosphere out there, just like down here on earth-I-C, and that we can live up there, and that transportation will be very important, so what? With your technology, you can figure out the transportation before he even gets there. The machine was made to be destroyed. There was nothing you could have done! Jane, I think you are more special than you think you are. Probably more special than anyone and everyone I know and will know. Now, can you please continue stroking? It feels amazing; don't stop!* Jane smiles and continues stroking his hair.

Sam continues, *Listen, I have been working on projects myself, a suit, and an energy sphere. I have a few designs at home. The suit was proven kind of useless because somehow I do have powers, everything I wanted to do with the suit, I can do now without it, I hope. We could work on it together for you! There is something you should know, though: I was kind of goofing around with it, and came up with a goofy design mechanism or something like that. At a specific speed with specific movements, of course, when it is activated, it plays melodies—something jazzy. We might need to get rid of that.* Sam pulls out his phone and plays different jazz songs to explain to her what kind of jazz he is talking about. Jane stops stroking and leans forward to look at his face. She says, *Sam! You are a genius! I haven't yet seen it, but I think it's amazing, and the problem with the song—let's not make it a problem. I want it to stay as an original concept. Let's keep it soft. When I'm trying to make my last move and start walking, it will be all JAZZ, JAZZ, JAZZ, JAZZ, you know? And it will remind me of one amazing thing, or someone.* she winks.

Sam laughs out loud and says, *Well, that was unexpected! What name should we give you in that suit?*

Silence...

They shout at the same time while looking at each other. *JAZZ!!!!!!*

Chapter 31

Jazz is the name of her new suit. The name comes from the special design and functionality of her suit. With a specific amount of energy and speed and with specific moves, the design will make the ribs and the middle section of the spinal area vibrate, creating different types of jazz cores. Soft or hardcore depends on the movements of the flaps.

They try creating a scary and overwhelming melody to frighten the enemy as she comes along. They eventually agree on one: It is not the matter of getting someone frightened. Rather, it is to give an enemy a taste of the beauty of peaceful harmony through music before being defeated.

Jane is looking forward to seeing Sam's design. She moves her head to the melody Sam is playing. She says, *Alright, this melody is dope! I like this one, and this one too. But, like I said, it needs to be a little softer. It's still super nice, though. Sam smiles at her and tells her that he already knows how dope it sounds. After all, he created it.

Hey, wanna see it right now?

Jane nods her head, and her eyes glow out of happiness. She trembles with joy and asks Sam if he is going to run her home.

Japp! That – is – what – we – gon-na – do!

Jane unlocks the last amount of energy in her suit to get it back online. She closes both the body armor and the helmet.

This time imma make sure I'm ready, just so I don't end up puking again, she says, laughing nervously.

Sam, already knowing she is right, gets on his feet and jumps like an athlete, warming up for his next run. He stretches his shoulders, then his armstrings, followed by his wrists, neck, and ankles.

Alright, this is going to be my best run ever! Maybe this time I will actually be able to slow down perfectly. All I have to keep in mind is lowering the speed much earlier than the destination determines, I need a new formula. You know what, Jane? You won't even feel us moving!, he says with confidence, stretching out his chest and looking straight ahead.

Both friends are ready. Jane jumps for him to carry her in his arms and holds tightly on his neck with her left hand.

Okay, let's goooo!, she shouts with a shivering tone.

Sam laughs at her and holds her arm and thigh tight with the right amount of pressure. He shouts, *alright, leeet's goooooooo!* with the "g" starting as soon as he takes his first step into the horizon.

Before Jane gets the chance to shout, *woo-hooo* they arrive in front of his front door. She lowers her mask as quickly as possible. Sam, as attentive as he is, quickly holds up her hair and raises a bucket to her face. She pukes.

I'll give you three out of ten points. This wasn't as awful as the first time. My suit can keep up a little bit. But I still haven't had enough time to process what's happening. Your running is really sloppy, dude! She says it with an awkward smile.

The same quickly changes the subject. He is curious about an event.

There is something about you that I have been worrying about. It happened on the same day my abilities were unlocked. The explosion changed something about you! I feel this kind of energy within you, not quite as unique as mine, but also not like a normal person. I need to observe and think further before I can explain anything. Plus, I have something that will be perfect for the suit, or at least the energy problem the suit will have. Two, to be precise. Anyways let's go upstairs. My designs are lying around in my workshop. Sam points this out before entering the building with her.

He shows her his entire gallery in his workshop, his bedroom. Every design he has ever made is stored here.

Sam! This is amazing! I think the last time I was here was at the very beginning, when you only had a sleeping bag and a kitchen. Everything you brought from your old apartment was just laying around because... Jane tells Sam. Sam is embarrassed by the fact that she spits it out. He says, *It wasn't THAT bad! I mean, here and there, there were a few things not stored as they are right now, but not THAT bad! And also, please don't just say it loudly like that! It's a little embarrassing, even though there has been some improvement in here.*

Jane is smiling at Sam. She thinks Sam being embarrassed is cute.

Come oon, Sam! It's just me! It's not like I'm your mom or a new girl you just met. It's kinda cute!, she says.

What is cute? Cuz I know I'm not! You being a girl makes it more awkward. Please, don't!

Jane walks into his bedroom and bounces on his bed. *Haaa*, she exhales loudly. She turns around and lays on her tummy. She pulls her arms towards her and folds those, placing her chin on them. She looks at Sam with the cutest smile while he walks into the room.

He is confused and asks, *you good?* Jane is smiling and raises her eyebrows. She raises and drops them several times, quickly. She answers, *jaaaap, I'm good! Never felt better, like literally! I love your apartment, by the way!* Sam gives her the thumbs up.

Sooo where is the suit's design? she asks.

Sam tells her that he is going to show them later and drops onto his bean bag. Suddenly, he disappears, and reappears from the ceiling, and falls in front of Jane after she sits back up after noticing the strange event.

What just happened, Sam? she asks.

Sam is just as confused as her. He doesn't know what, why, or how... It just happened. He comes to the conclusion that it is a kind of space travel. He says, *I think I might have just space-time traveled. Or was it just space travel? Wait, you were on your tummy as I jumped. How long was I gone for?*

Jane tells him, *It should be around fifteen seconds. You were gone for fifteen seconds, Sam! I thought it was some kind of trick, but then you came down from the ceiling! That's dope! You unlocked something new! You have to do it again! How did you do it?*

Sam strokes his goatie and says, *Well, I was falling back, and while looking at the ceiling, I thought about how much fun it would be if I could fall from up there. I wanted to see something awesome, like the floor, and my - my chair and stuff*

The truth is, he was thinking about looking at Jane's behind from the ceiling's point of view.

He feels exhausted from the jump but decides not to tell Jane about it.

Space travel: Traveling to destinations through space. It takes time to reappear, seconds, minutes, or even hours. The time depends on the user's skills and experience. Space-time travel: The user travels to a destination without having time pass by "instatanous teleportation." The user arrives at the very moment he teleports.

Wow, so you just have to imagine a destination. Let's try this. But this time, I will tell you what you need to do. I have been having these theories about fiction for a very long time. I think I know exactly what to do. She says and continues, *First of all, we need to travel as much as possible, and you have to have every surroundings you will always discover in your brain; you have to memorize and analyze everything! Cuz you having to imagine places means that you need to have been at the exact spot and you have to know your exact position. Let Jazz teach you!* She stands on Sam's right-hand side in front of his bedroom door and tells him, *Alright, now just think of my garage. You've been there before. It doesn't matter where exactly we appear; it just has to be in my garage, where nothing is in your way.* She holds his arm as tightly as possible and tells him not to forget her.

Done, I think I know where we are going now!. He says. Before he takes the first step forward, Jane asks him, *So what is the deal with boys and urinals? Like I know they mostly go alone, but what do they do when they are all gathered at once? Do they urinate simultaneously into one pisoir? Or do they just chill and talk with one another like girls in the women's washroom?*

Chapter 32

Sam and Jane travel through space and appear in a cabinet at the very end of the women's washroom.

Whaaaaaat?!?! Jane shouts right before she covers Sam's mouth with both hands. She asks him why they aren't in Jane's bedroom. Sam mumbles. After all, his mouth is covered.

Jane asks, *Our being here means that you have been here before, am I right? What were you doing in here?*

She let's go of Sam's mouth, allowing him to answer the question.

Umm, I was here not too long ago. I needed to urinate really badly, and the boy's washroom was full, so I decided to release my liquids here as there were no girls inside after I yelled out, asking if there was someone in here.

He continues...

But why the hell did you come up with the question? You know, you can be really random at times!

He laughs loudly, pulls Jane, and takes a leap forward.

They reappear in Jane's bedroom.

*It worked! Jane, it worked! We are here! You were right! Oh man, you are a genius! He shouts and kisses her on the left cheek.

Awkward silence...

Jane blushes.

Sam holds her hand tightly. They travel back to his room.

He jumps onto his bed and takes a deep breath. His sweat is noticeable.

Sam, are you sweating? she asks.

Sam's forehead and armpits are soaked with sweat, and he is shaking.

He has the worst cramps ever!

He tries playing cool to convince Jane that everything is alright. She, however, doesn't believe a word he is saying. She argues, *Bro, you are out of breath and sweating like hell. You can't tell me this is a normal thing for you. Cuz you, ma guy, you aren't feeling well. Or is it because of the women's washroom? Wait, is it because it was something you would rather not let anyone know? Awww, you are embarrassed! We could just pretend I never knew a thing. Though it really won't be easy to forget you had to use the women's washroom, hahaha!* She laughs hesterically.

Sam is embarrassed. He moans out of pain and asks her to get him some magnesium pills and a glass of water. He explains to her that it is never the reason why he is weak.

I'm almost all dried out. It takes too much energy to jump. I don't think it's a skill I want to be using frequently, or at all! My body can't withstand the stress. Imma stick to the traditional running stuff. One day, I should be fast enough to break the barrier through speed. Theoretically, it shouldn't drain that much energy.

Jane sits on the floor and tries to make sense of what Sam says. She nods slowly and agrees, *I think you are right, Sam! I mean, doing it just like this is like pressing a saw against the object you are trying to cut. Now, should the saw not be sharp enough, this would mean that you would damage it. But with the right amount of speed and precision, it all becomes easier. This makes a saw for wood capable of "harming" metal.*

Sam is impressed by her example. For an uncountable, forgotten amount of time, he tells her how amazing her way of thinking is.

Quick to understand and quick to find an easier explanation. Damn, you amaze me more every time we hang out.

Jane blushes intensively.

She giggles, curls her hair behind her right ear, and says, *jeeez, always quick with those compliments. You're making me blush right now. Thank you!*

She adds, *So our next mission is to make a Speedy Gonzalez out of you, or maybe rather, Sonic!*

Nah, something more like The Flash!

They both laugh as they never would have thought of having such a conversation—a conversation about training themselves to become exactly like comic-sci-fi characters.

They fast-forward and talk about Sam's design. Jane notices something strange about a component. Sam has been working on a battery, an energy source, but it's like none other.

His project is called the sphere, or the energy sphere. This creation is to be one of the greatest achievements known to mankind.

The energy sphere is a self-sustaining energy source that is born with a specific amount of energy input. The energy added helps the sphere glow and charge up to one-tenth of the maximum energy it can give out. One-tenth of the energy built up is stored and sustained as long as it isn't connected to a circuit. Opening the circuit gives an output signal right through the sphere's core, making it charge up to one hundred and ten percent of the energy needed. This happens in less than 5 milliseconds. The sphere glows from white to blue, signaling that the goal has been reached. The second part of the sphere's circuit is either built in the host device or on the outside of a massive machine or a building. This part is called the sustainer.

What does the sustainer do?

The sustainer is to keep the energy flow stable. It works partly like a capacitor and stores energy. Precisely, the excessive energy being produced. With it, the sphere works with the same amount of energy for hours or days without interruption.

Imagine the sphere shooting energy into the upper part of the sustainer. The sustainer stores it and turns it into electricity; this happens in the middle part of the sustainer. The electricity then passes through the lower part, which is divided into two parts: one for the device and one connected to the sphere.

The part connected to the sphere stores the energy as long as the sphere is working over one hundred percent. As soon as the capacity drops to ninety-nine point nine percent, the sustainer works at one hundred percent efficiency. It sucks out energy, making the sphere drop to eighty-five percent for approximately ninety-five milliseconds.

During this time, it compresses the new stored energy, passes through the lower part, and shoots it back into the sphere's core. The compressed energy shot into the core gives it a „shock," keeping it stable for the next cycle.

A cycle starts and ends with a compressed shock. Depending on the size of both the sphere and the device it gives power to, the cycle should end between forty-eight and fifty-six hours.

The core needs maintenance after four hundred and fifty-six cycles when in use throughout days without a resting phase, or exactly three years if the limit of cycles hasn't been achieved yet.

The sphere can be connected to a device without being used. This phase is called the snooze-phase or standby. Here, it is activated, but with a one-thousandth of effectiveness.

All these theories and calculations, Sam has already done. His only problem is his lack of raw-materials and perfect technology. Jane is his only solution. Her invention of lightweight, wireless technology is the only thing missing in his plan, and she knows exactly how to solve it. She uses all her equipment and money to help Sam with his best invention ever.

Well, right after the suit, of course!

After two months, they create the first energy sphere. It makes little to no sound at all. The sustainer gets a new name, the crown. They adjust it to Jane's new and improved suit. She suits up and feels energy surging all around her. All her senses are magnified, and Sam's modification to her helmet helps her brain accelerate in a healthy way without hurting any part of her body. The suit is soft but hard as soon as it senses dangerous forces. She can jump from one roof to the next with ease.

After half a year, Sam has become more confident with his speed. His running is less sloppy, and he can transport living creatures without hurting them, though he has to run slower to do so. Together with Jane, he creates an inversion of the energy sphere. The sphere is attached to Sam's vest (an invention from Jane) to be charged while he is running to help him keep his powers in tact and have a backup power plan for Jane. Both friends train together and become stronger. Jane uses her suit and fighting skills to fight crimes and arouses the world's military's attention. She gets a bounty and has competitors chasing after her:

Wanted: Dead Species: Alien/Supernatural Name: Jazz Bounty: 22,061,999 Ranal coins

Sam tells Jane about the possibility of being able to travel through space and time. Jane commits herself to a new project to help him. She decides to work alone until she discovers a solution. Sam, bored and somehow motivated, takes on Jane's role as Jazz and runs throughout continents with a fake version of her suit created just for him, with less technology. The only high-tech device he carries is a vest and an inverted energy sphere to power up.

A few months into playing Jazz...

Sam runs to a crime scene. He is lazy and takes a shortcut. He runs through a school's sports field, where he sees a boy glowing. There are wings popping out of his back, creating a shockwave that blows every kid around him away. He slows down and helps out the boy and his friends.

Being distracted by the boy's questioned face, he unintentionally lets his guard down and shows him a part of his face for a split second.

His energy is sucked up by the boy. It makes him arrive too late at the crime scene. Five innocent lives are taken in front of his eyes, but he manages to capture the murderers. This event makes him question his existence. He remains depressed...

But he never shows...

...until Jane announces her good news.

Saaam! I've done it! Look at what I created! It's gonna cost you an immense amount of energy to use it, but it will be worth it, trust me! We are going to space travel!

Chapter 33

Later in the year 2041.

Inside the largest state prison at twenty-three hundred hours...

Hey, Jin! Do you remember me? Imagine me with longer hair!

Jin's eyes widen.

Is it...you? How did you? Wait, where is Silvester? What about...? What happened?

As always, asking of him first, even now that I'm the only one standing right in front of you. Don't you think it's... how do I say it nicely? Disrespectful?

Jin lowers his head. He apologizes and asks, *How have you been?*

Thanks! But... It doesn't change a thing, does it now?

Jin is happy to see his old friend again.

The first thing he observes...

Hey, the way you speak has changed. It's much more modern than it used to be, ahhahahahahahaha... haaaa. He laughs.*So you have learned a lot throughout the years, it seems. How are you visiting me now and not earlier? Not to be rude or something*

Well, you have been gone for a while now. I never sensed you until a few weeks ago. The real question is, when did you come back? I thought you were gone for good...

Jin smiles. He looks up to the roof and says, *The time has finally come. My descendants—one of them, though he is... was young—somehow helped me. I was captured in-between time for ions. I was actually always there. Just, human. It's much more complicated than that. Still, you know my name. You could've tried something! Like finding me?*

But I'm here now, or? I have a favor to ask you. We could make a deal and work together; what do you say?

Jin scratches his scalp intensively.

What is it? What do you need? I'm not that rich, but I'll try my best.

Don't worry, Money, I do have more than enough! Well, let's say it has something to do with your descendants...

These exact words are something Jin has never thought to hear about. He is deeply surprised. He has no other choice but to ask what it's all about.

Lucius; his name is Lucius. This guy and his friend Blu... Oh, and HE wants someone specific out of the picture; his name is Sam.

Huh?

Jin doesn't know who Sam is.

I haven't met anyone with that name yet. What do you mean by "HE and him?" Why is it this specific person?

Silence...

Jin has a bad feeling about the situation. He asks again, *Who the hell is HE? What is his name? Wait, you are half a god. Why don't you just take whoever it is out? Shouldn't you be strong enough to defend yourself? You are suspicious, dude! You are scared of him! I can see fear in your eyes.*

I don't care what you think! He takes a deep breath to calm down. Suddenly, Jin doesn't see any kind of emotion in his eyes.

He pulls toward Jin and looks closely. He stares him in the eyes and tells him, *He wants him out of the picture, and so be it. I've got to do everything in my power to grant HIM his wish. There is no escaping for me! and there is no letting HIM down!*

The cell is filled with negative energy. By asking for the third time, Jin disapproves of not getting an answer. He stands up to attack.

Silence...

He looks into his palms. His face defines anxiety and confusion. He waves his hand over his head and claps. His anxious face is more intense as he asks, *What the hell is wrong with my powers? Why can't I activate them?*

**You have been sitting in this cell for months and years. Are you trying to tell me that you haven't ever tried using them in here? Impressive, dude! Alright, let me explain this to you—not that it really mattered until now, though: I constructed this cell to hold back your powers. I have studied your Tomei ever since I decided to leave you guys. First, I learned to suppress my energy to the level of an ant and kept spying on you. One could say that you aren't powerful enough to sense an ant doing his business. Tomei is a very tricky concept, but yours is literally hell. Lucky for me, it is not that powerful. I needed to use every piece of information I had collected from the years you spent throughout time. Waiting for you to reappear in time made me hate you even more. Your problem is simple to explain: within these walls, your powers are bye-bye. Mine, however, are still here.*

He smashes Jin against the wall. His anger intensifies as he looks into Jin's face and tells him, *I will tell you the story, so listen carefully!*

He pulls Jin and tosses him against the wall behind him. He walks towards the bed and sits on it.

*After you disappeared, I came out of my hiding space to help Silvester. We fought Thor for days until he was weak enough for me to absorb his energy, which I did. Surprisingly, or not so surprising at all, now that I look back into it, the absorption made me stronger. I became strong enough to give him the final blow. After that, I sliced off his limbs and ate them. I made both Silvester, who had to rest, and Thor himself, who wasn't dead yet, watch me eat them all. I absorbed his remainings and merged with them. Thor was powerful. I'm talking about crazy powerful! It took me weeks to get used to controlling his will. Years after years, we were hoping to see you. We never did.

Silvester was so sure that you would never come back to us. He told me you had to be reborn and awaken at some point because of this time travel thing you guys kept bragging about. He and I traveled around to spread your and Anansi's names. Apparently, it had to be something really important, and he had promised to do so. I did everything I could, and I got stronger. Somehow Silvester kept growing stronger and stronger, faster than me. It made me so sick. I envied him, and I hoped that one could give me some advice. I asked him to travel with us through time to the point where you awakened. Maybe not that far, but somewhere near that time.

He said you guys came from a further future, so I asked to jump a couple steps; he refused! I got the idea to create something amazing. Something where someone at the top could help improve the lower beings. Of course, he told me I was manifesting a god complex from my dad to control everything. I never truly understood what it meant; after I understood the meaning of it, I still didn't understand what he was trying to tell me. All I knew was that he was holding back my potential. What did I do, you may ask?*

He waits for Jin to ask him this question.

Jin sighs and asks, *So what did you do?*

Interesting question! He replies.

I looked around and studied him to find his weakness. After 10 years, I was ready. I was almost as strong as him because his capacity was full.Yes, it exists! There is a maximum capacity we can hold. Some have larger, others don't.

He stretches his arms apart and smiles at Jin.

I killed him! I gave him the idea of creating shadow creatures. A forbidden technique, it seems. I saw the danger and made him do it anyway for him to be weak enough, and then...

He slides his thumb across his neck and laughs.

Jin sheds tears and breaks his cup with brute strength. He asks, *You killed him??*

Japp! I almost regretted it, but after ten generations, this guy named Jamie was born. I sensed his potential. A potential that would help me achieve my goals. I laid the path for him to grow powerful. I waited for his sixty-first birthday and introduced myself. After a few years, we became something like besties. I was best friends with Silvester's descendant!

He stands up, turns around, and sits on the ground to continue.

*We walked the globe to explore. I learned a few more things. Jamie's capacity was extra large! At some point, I thought it was finally time to fulfill my dream. I asked him to create what we now call the government, but he refused. Just like his greeeeaaaat grandfather. I couldn't defeat him, even though I knew his weakness. That's how strong he was. I started creating the government plan in secret until I got my own strong followers. I threatened to kill his people because I knew he couldn't stop all of us at once.His weakness was standing in burning blue flames with his aura locked away. His aura, I made him seal into a box, which he hid away from me, that bastard!

He was allowed to have enough Tomei so he could see. He was a naturally blind person, and I mean, I'm not a monster to kill him without letting him see his last moments. He stood in the fire and looked right into my eyes. Somehow, after an hour, he was still alive, so I helped out the flames a little bit. It changed the flame's color to blue; that was how I found out it had to be a blue flame full of Tomei energy. I was lucky that no one saw or had suspicions.I announced my rulership and made everyone work under me to pay me. I made them think all the money was to pay the workers, but most of it I kept and made sure that the countries on my continent were in debt to keep the payments going. Other countries took my example and created their own; I managed to conquer a few of them too.

I went ahead and broke our deal. I killed every clan member of his. Unfortunately, not all. It seems the others found out and played smart games. Long story short, the others who got away kept giving birth to new offspring. Blu and Lucius are the strongest ones left, and I don't like it. I want them gone, and I think only you can do it. Anyways, A few years ago, someone mighty summoned me. I have never met anyone this powerful. Not even my Zeus is that powerful. This god hides his body in the shadows and his face in the light. He calls himself Time. He doesn't like repeating himself, it seems. And all he wants is for this Sam dude to be gone. That's also something you can do. Take all three out of the picture, and you might as well be free from this space.*

Jin sighs and looks to the ground. He tells him that he doesn't trust him and asks, *So why do you want Blu and Lucius out of the story?*

Well, I once sent this useless guy to take care of some scientists, and he messed up. They were successful with their project and gave the most important one to their biological son, who has spoken to Blu and Lucius about the situation; they might be looking for me to take revenge. My goal was to find a way to make normal people supernatural and create an army. I need an army to take down the other governments. If I do everything alone, no one will ever trust me, so it is the only way, and like I said, they are in my way. So, what do you say? You in?

Jin laughs at him and gives him a direct answer: *No! Never! Nein! Niemals!*

Well then, it seems I have to do everything by myself as quickly as possible before things get out of hand. Maybe I am that monster. You will see! I will make sure you feel it and regret your decision! After that, I will make sure your sentence is much longer. I will make sure none ever finds out that it was your uncle who killed your sister, and not you!

He smiles and walks off gently, leaving Jin angry for the very first time.

Hey!!!!! Don't! Stop that! Leave them alone!!!! Don't you dare touch them or anything about my case! Hey! Come back here! Don't you dare! I mean it!!!! If you ever... Come back here, Morphius!!!!

Chapter 34

On a cultivated field in North Philsway...

It is November, and even though it's almost winter, the first two weeks of the month are hot.

Sam is laying on a plain field behind town, working on his abilities. With the air compressed into a ball, he adds driplets of water as the core and plays with it. He throws it up in the air and moves it around by swirling around his fingers.

Ok, now, without stopping the ball, I've gotta concentrate on expanding my senses. First, compress an amount into my chest.

He tries this out and succeeds after ten minutes.

Perfect! He is happy that it's working just as he wants it to.

Now let it out slowly! Just like I did it last time!

He refills the energy as he lets it out. He sustains the outlet. By compressing and refilling, he manifests a visible object. He duplicates the air-water ball he had before. This time it isn't made from his surroundings; it is a manifestation of an object through Tomei energy. He trains his senses by adjusting god's seventh sense. His eyes are closed. Everything he does, he sees through his now-passive skill. For the first time, he looks into the sky lands.

Wow, those are beautiful!

He senses a company behind him. It' Blu!

Hey, how you doing, Blu?

Blu walks towards him and takes a seat on the ground.

What's that, Sam?

Sam smirks.

Oh, it's just this awesome ball I just created. Beautiful, isn't it?

Blu is stunned and asks Sam if he is allowed to hold it for a minute.

Sure, why not? Coat your fingers with water and think fast!

Blu reaches out for Sam's water bottle and coats his fingers with it. His abilities help him maintain the amount of water and its elasticity.

Sam quickly throws the ball with a strong force, making it difficult for Blu to catch it. He catches it anyway. He tilts the ball in all directions and asks Sam, *Since when do you have powers? It's been a really long time since we last met, hasn't it, Cousin?*

Yeah... Wait, hol up! Sasm interrupts.

You just saw me doing something extraordinary, and all you ask is, „Since when do you have powers?" You aren't surprised at all!

Blu smiles and looks at his cousin. He tells him he already knows because he has it himself. *I mean, you knew I was there, even though I was abnormally quiet and your eyes were closed. Not even the craziest concentration could have noticed me! I thought you already knew about me.*

Sam replies, *No, not really!* He is interested in a conversation with his younger cousin.

Blu reminds him that he has always talked about how cool superpowers will be if he has them.

He continues, *All your theories, I tried them out and they worked, so I thought you already had the idea, didn't you? The entire time? When did you first notice your powers?*

Sam drops his smile.

Exactly one week after we met for the last time. I never had them; they were gifted to me. Long story! And no, I never knew about it. Does your family know?

Blu nods.

And no one ever bothered to give me information. My entire life, everyone thought I was this crazy dude. They looked at me like I was crazy because of what I thought was possible. Everyone knew it was possible and never said a thing. Keeping secrets from me as always. You know, mostly I say it is all good, but the truth is, I am not. I worked hard to push away many feelings and emotions. Just so that no one pitties me. Whatever... What's done is done. There is no going back now, is there? I don't need to lose my temper now that I have finally learned to dissolve it. Plus, you have nothing to do with it. You were too young to know what was happening

A warm breeze flushes over their skin, making their silence awkward. Sam asks his cousin what type of abilities he has.

To be honest with you, I don't know. I'd like it to be a bit of everything. He puts on a cute smile.

Lately, I have been able to move water a bit. First it was air, then a little bit of fire. I am able to counter Lucius', my best friend's, fire attack. Maybe it's because his flames aren't strong enough. He keeps burning himself up before generating a stronger flow.

Sam takes off the thermoscarf covering his eyes and opens them. The heat between the scarf and his skin is released, causing vapor to come out of it. He raises his hand with the scarf tied around it and asks Blu, *Your best friend also has powers? There are more of you guys?*

Jap! There are more of us. One new classmate, who I want to be friends with, also has powers. His energy is a little bit weird. I sense it, but somehow he is different from us. It doesn't feel normal. His aura feels fragile, but it looks powerful and scary. It's like he's fighting for his life or something. But he hasn't mastered his skills yet. My best friend, however... I think he is stronger than me, and I want us to be stronger together, but ever since the incident from last time, he has been pushing me away. He says he doesn't want anything to do with me, that he is better off alone, and everyone, including me, sucks, but there is more to it. I think he is trying to push me away because he is afraid to lose or hurt me. Do you think you could help me out? Like, help me understand him?

Sam tilts his head to the right, trying to think about something. He sits and crosses his legs. He asks Blu when the „incident" has happened.

I don't remember that much, but a few weeks after that, this bounty poster of someone called Jazz showed up. It made him angrier and frightened! You know? He is not that kind of person to get frightened of someone like that. I hope someone finds Jazz and locks him or her away. I need my best friend back. Unfortunately, I don't think anyone is good enough to catch him if he is still out there.

uhhmm Blu?

Sup? Blu answers.

About that... Are you talking about that time where you guys fell to the ground with the explosion and stuff?

Yeah... Wait, how do you know about that? Blu's eyes widened as he asks.

Well, because I was there. I dropped you guys to the ground.

Blu draws himself closer.

You dropped us? But why? And you didn't say hello! Had you forgotten about me?

Sam laughs out of embarrassment. He explains to his cousin that there is a lot going on in his life. He continues, *You wouldn't believe what I had to deal with the past couple of months... There is a reason why your friend hates or is frightened of Jazz. That's because Jazz saved him. He was deadly and dangerous, and he had to find out the hard way that there is more going on in this world. Long talking cut short, I am Jazz! Well, a part of Jazz.*

He rolls his eyeballs to the right side and squints both his lips and nose.

So what next? Do you hate me too? Are you going to turn me in?

Chapter 35

It's been a while since Sam has asked Blu what he wants to do with the information given to him.

Blu? Blu!?!

Blu gives off the cutest smile and tells Sam that there is no reason to betray him.

Now that I know that it was you, I don't hate Jazz anymore. I mean, you had your reasons. And after all that you just told me, I have the feeling that Lucius is just a drama queen. Jazz did nothing wrong to make him THIS mad! The news shows this awesome suit of yours. Did you make it yourself?

Sam's smile ends in laughter. He feels a heavy load lifted off of his shoulders.

You see, theoretically, Jazz is not just me, you know? We are two people. It's kinda funny that no one has ever noticed the difference between us. I mean, boobs and no boobs?! I guess we are this awesome, perfect team, don't you think so?

Blu is confused; he asks himself why he claims there are two people. Since when does he have friends—in this context, a girl friend. Sam isn't the type to hang around a girl that much. He knows Sam as the guy who is too shy to have a normal conversation with a woman. He only speaks to or has relationships with women who claim to be his friends and speak to him first. His nervousness around women is extreme!

You... and a girl? He asks.

Blu still doesn't believe it. He asks, *Are you some kind of "Venom" thing? Or is your suit like some living thing or whatever?* He laughs awkwardly.

WE... ARE... VENOM...

Sam jokes around with Blu's "ridiculous" idea.

Come on, man! For real? Ight, maybe all this superpower stuff is true and stuff, but come on, aliens? I have never in my life seen one before, so... I can't say.

The boys stand up and walk around. They joke around for a while until Sam decides to reply to Blu's question.

With „we," I mean me and my friend Jane.

Ouhhh, a girl friend... Your gilfriend? You have a girl? You like girls? You can, love? I thought you were a robot or something, especially since the last time we met. You have become less boring, dude!

Sam smiles out of embarrassment and eventually bursts out in laughter. He looks around to check if someone is watching or listening to their conversation.

Wait a second, I thought you didn't need to turn around to see something?!

Sam laughs awkwardly.

Blu gives him a side eye and says sarcastically, *I ain't judging you... nooope!*

He moves towards Sam, making him uncomfortable.

Geesh, boy, give me some space now, would you? She is a.. Girl... Friend! And not MY girlfriend, alright? We have been good friends for a while now, and we are both students. At least she was. We are not from the exact same uni, but we have a similar curriculum. Even if I liked her that much, which I don't! There is no chance for me to have her. I don't think I'm on her level. She is way above my league. She is beautiful, smart, rich—her family, naturally beautiful, kind, whatever—shut up!

Blu laughs loudly. He holds his tummy and drops to the ground after smacking Sam on the shoulder. After a few minutes, he gains control and takes a deep breath.

Hey, look! If you want her that bad, why don't you just tell her and see what happens? What could go wrong? The worst that can happen is her saying "no." Besides, why would you bother? You are powerful now. You can do anything you want and go everywhere you want. I don't think a single girl can make you fall so hard. There are beautiful ones out there, one of which you might like more. You know, a soulmate!? Blu, as young as he is, lectures Sam.

Sam stops and sits on the ground in the middle of an abandoned road. His cousin, after walking for a while, notices him not by his side and walks back to him. He takes a seat in front of him and asks, *What is wrong?*

I don't know; well, maybe I do. I may like her, a bit. I don't want to rush anything, though. The last time I gave in to feelings, it hit me hard. You know how much I struggled to get myself back together. I gained weight, couldn't sleep well, kept on eating without a break, and so on. I can't let it happen again! And after all that I have made myself into, I don't deserve such happiness. I have brought myself to hate human beings. I don't have any feelings towards them. I don't have the urge to help or save them. Everything I have gone through lately has only been about me. I plan and think forward through everything to achieve just my goals, nothing more. Do you really think that someone like me deserves love and happiness from someone else except myself?

Blu sighs and slaps his forehead before flicking Sam's. He says, *What happened to my crazy, normal, boring cousin? Now all that's left is boring boring! Stop saying stupid things. Look at you! If someone desires a perfect life, it should be you! Also, you are kind, handsome, tall... enough, funny, boring... Your heart is in the right place! I don't know what has happened to you ever since the last time, and I don't care, but let it go. It's time for you to open yourself up once more and see what happens. Or could it be that you are afraid you will lose your friendship if it all gets messed up? Are you afraid to lose a friend? That's new!*

Me?, pff Sam plays it off elegantly. So he thinks.

Afraid to lose a friend? Good one! It seems you have already taken over my role of telling jokes!

He stares at Blu and hopes for an answer, but gets none.

He continues, *Ok, yeah, maybe just a bit. I don't want to lose her, I think. She is the first person who has made me unsure of leaving or not leaving. She is the only girl I might run after if something goes wrong. I haven't talked to her in a long while, too. Anyways, she is the original Jazz. I have taken over her role until she is done with a project we have taken on ourselves. Ever since she told me she was almost done with it and hugged me and kissed me, I haven't talked to her. I don't know if I should go to her place or not.*

Blu is curious and asks Sam if she is superhuman.

Not really; there is something new going on with her but she isn't a supe. Her suit is designed for her to be that powerful. It is of our creation. Impressive, isn't it?

There is a short period of uncomfortable silence before Blu answers, *Sure!*

He lays down and crosses his legs while placing his hands underneath the back of his head. He tells Sam, *I'm not trying to barge into some kind of relationship between two adults. Sorry, one woman and a young dude. After all, I'm just a kid, a young teenager who has been taught a lot from his cousin in his younger years. Everything coming from me was taught to me by you. Remember when you told me that I was your insurance for the days you lose your way?*

Thank you! Sam interrupts to appreciate Blu.

Yeah, yeah, sure! Anyways, you are dragging her into matters in which she might not survive. You do know that if something is to happen to her anytime soon, it will be your doing? If she dies, the blood stains will be on your hands. And there is no escaping this fact. You having feelings for her will make it less good. You know that, right? Have you been able to keep your promise?

Yes! I never break my promise, ever! You know me!

Blu gives him a long, *MMHMMMM*, and continues, *Was just checking. Exactly this mindset makes you my role model. Back to the point... If something is to happen to her, do you think you will be able to keep exactly what makes your promise bond stable? Do you think you can move on without regretting any decision you have made so far?*

Sam, without hesitation, answers, *Yes! It will hurt me really bad because it will be the second time I lose someone without confessing or trying to take her out on a real date. But, regretting that she is like this and that something happens because of this exact decision is not an option. Sooner or later, I might live through it; I will survive! I mean, surviving is what I have been doing my entire life, alone! I'm trying to finally let someone in, and I think it might not be bad not to be alone. If this means letting the person decide for himself what he likes and desires and truly accepting that decision, then so be it. This time, I'm going to let go of control.*

Blu smiles at his cousin. He is filled with satisfaction. *That's exactly the answer I've been looking for! You are still yourself. Now, take your own advice and let her decide. Tell her what you feel!*

Maybe someday, when my confidence boosts. Right now, we've gotta figure out how to manipulate worlds. And I have to train and become strong enough to generate enough power. Maybe you would like to do some workouts with me?

Blu sits back up. *Yes! Train me, cousin! Please! I want to travel around worlds with you. It's gonna be awesome!* He is happy to have a chance to spend more time with his favorite cousin. Apparently, Sam is the man he looks up to and likes the most.

No, Blu! I'll travel with her alone! Maybe next time. It's settled, then. I will be your sensei! He puts a convincing smile on his face.

They drift off of their topic, tell each other jokes, and laugh out loud. After a while, they walk back to the fields and work on concentrating their energy.

Hey Sam! What a coincidence! You also hang out here?!

Both boys look at each other, to her, and back at each other. Blu asks, *Why is that girl shouting at us? Do you know her? Who is she? Is that the girl you were talking about? Jane?!?*

Blu widely opens his mouth as he is surprised to see a woman as beautiful as her calling his cousin formally.

Chapter 36

✱ Is that Jane? Damn, cousin! She is beau-ti-ful! Why didn't you mention how beautiful she is? Come on, now!*

Sam looks to the side and looks at Blu without moving his head. He asks him, *For real?*

Jane walks closer. She asks them about how they are doing and says once more, *It's been a while, Sam! I have texted a few times now and still got no answer. Are you okay? You look okay!*

Yeah, I'm good. Just been dealing with some stuff. I think I'm alright now; don't worry.

She looks at Sam suspiciously.

She has been worried about him for a while, and he is saying everything is alright without smiling for a second. She believes Sam will tell her if he is ready and doesn't want to push him.

„Sometimes keeping a secret is the best option." She remembers a quote Sam has once told her.

Alright, I'm going to pretend to believe it for now. I have news, good and bad. The bad one, you are not going to like! She announces.

What is it? Sam and Lucius both ask and draw closer to her.

She asks Sam who the *"cute little boy"* is, and he explains their relationship to her: *He is my cousin, my favorite cousin, to be precise. We haven't heard from each other for a while now. The last time was weeks before the „incident."

He turns to Blu and introduces his friend: *Blu, this is Jane.*

Hi, Blu!

Hi, Jane! They shake hands before Jane pulls him in for a hug.

Blu is surprised. *A hugger... nice!*

He continues, *Wow, you are very beautiful! I love your eyes! No wonder Sam keeps bragging and talking about you!*

Soo, Jazz? He whispers in her ears.

Jane smiles and blushes like never before. She says, *Wow, aren't you a cute little one?! So, Sam has been bragging about me? That's new, hahaha. Am I That amazing? What does he say?*

Blu laughs and tells Jane, *Well, he...*

One more word, Blu, and you're done! Your sensei will be leaving you! Sam interrupts.

Jane bursts out in laughter, *Alright, alright. Wait, sensei? Are you his teacher? Wow, Sam, I really haven't seen you in a while... What are you teaching him?*

Blu answers for Sam: *He is teaching me to control my powers and stuff. We started today.*

Jane's eyes widen. *Hmm? You also have powers?*

Sure! Blu says with confidence. Jane can't believe her ears. First, she never has believed in the supernatural, and then her best friend is blessed with them. Now even his little cousin is a supernatural being. She believes there can be no more surprises.

Is it a family thing? Does this mean there are millions, or maybe billions, of gifted human beings among us? Man, I'd love to gain just a single ability too! She says it with her saddest voice.

Sam looks at her with a serious face. He holds her shoulders and tells her that there is something important he needs to tell her. But first, she has to tell the good and bad news.

Yeah, sorry. Alright, good news first! I think the device is done. You know what I'm talking about! How we are going to use it depends on you, but I have a theory on how it should work. It's a navigation and power problem.

And the bad news? Blu asks curiously.

I have been researching and going through documents, conversations, and stuff from my dad since I didn't know if Sam was doing something or if he'd like to do something differrent...

Sorry about that. I'll try my best to not do such things in the future. Sam apologizes.

Jane asks him to promise, but he refuses.

She continues, *I see... Anyways, I found out about a conversation about this dude, who is nothing like a normal person. My dad has also been investigating behind everyone else's back to find out more. His documents state that my dad has been traveling, and throughout this travel stuff, he always met this guy just chilling, like everywhere. Once, he saw him leaving his seat, and he decided to take samples of his DNA as he had been touching everything on his chair.

He examined it and found no results. The test results had particles from a very far past; he is just one third human, whatever that means. It had the residues of other individuals in it too. He could only pick out one of the many individuals. And you won't believe it; it traces back to a boy called Lucius King and a man called Jin Fangs. The results point out that they are so old that it can't be this Lucius dude, so he stopped investigating. His diary says it is all just fiction, doesn't make sense, and is therefore a useless time waste. But That Jin Fangs is accurate. It's just...*

Lucius King... I know him! Blu shouts out.

Isn't he your best friend who hates Jazz because I saved him? Sam adds.

Blu confirms Sam's statement: *Yes, that's him, and he has been telling me stories about an ancestor of his. He says this man was burned alive but somehow disappeared in those flames, and no one knows how or why. He also keeps blabbering about being a descendant of the Monkey King. You know, this fictional character with the staff?*

There must be some truth behind it! Sam thinks. Jane tells them that she has been investigating Jin Fangs.

He has been imprisoned for some years now, and through my investigations, I found out that he is actually innocent. I have submitted every piece of proof I could find to free him and his friends, who were also falsely accused of murder. I visited the true murder of his sister, who is his uncle. I talked to him for hours. It seems he wanted to turn himself in, but someone forced him not to. He described what this man looked like, and we compared them to my father's files. It turns out it is the same ghost guy. He is afraid to handle things on his own and has asked me to leave it be, but...

Let me guess, you won't, and you want to visit Jin Fangs, right? Sam asks her.

Blu smiles suspiciously and looks left and right into Sam and Jane's faces.

I want to come too! Let's go and visit Jin!

Chapter 37

An hour after discussing the situation, Jane, Blu, and Sam visit the Monk-eye-King Prison in Valdes, an hour ride on the upstate train. Blu suspects something fishy about the prison's name and points out some obvious information.

Monk-eye-King prison: Is the name supposed to say something about the Monkey King? But why does it have a second e in it? Maybe it is supposed to mean something different?

Well, that was exactly my thought on that one. The only logical explanation was that it was built after something the Monkey King built. First I was like, "Maybe the Monkey King was once captured here, but no! This building is only forty years old. I don't think that dude is immortal, or? Well, now that I know that literally anything might be possible, it is safe to assume that the Monkey King truly lived and made awesome creations. Thus, this building is an unfinished structure he wanted to finish, and someone ended the job. Jane explains.

Sam, however, isn't going with Jane's idea. He adds, *But the Monkey King lived ions of years ago. I don't think he had that much modern technology or modern architectural skills to plan something like this. Even if he had planned something of a kind with that old-age technology of his, who could have possibly found his blueprints and know how to improve it all to fit our time? I heard that he hasn't been heard of since the deadliest event in history. Maybe the name is just to show how much power it holds. I mean, legends say that he has defeated an enormous number of gods. Wait, if it is a personification of his existence, would that mean entering the building means losing your powers? Could it be that the building can contain a godlike figure, just like he did? It will make us defenseless! How do we find out without it being too late?*

Quit whining!! Jane orders. She calms him down by explaining to him how strong he was before getting his abilities. *It's not like anyone is going to attack us just because we are entering. The plan is to visit Jin and his friends, have a talk with them, and then get out—nothing more!! According to what I found out, he should be in cell minus two-one-eight-three.*

What do those numbers mean, Jane? Blu asks. *minus two means underground on the second underground floor. There are a total of three underground floors and two above. One is the first department, eight means cell-room eight, and three is just on which cell floor.*

Sam nods and tells them to move faster.

The receptionist tells Jane to go inside and stops Sam and Blu.

Why? If I may ask. Jane doesn't understand why the boys aren't led in.

While the woman explains what her reasons are, it is clear: racism, a policy held by the prison. Dark-skinned people like Blu, who is lighter than Sam and lightly darker than Jane, do not enter the lower floors. His curly hair doesn't go unrecognized. Jane argues with her and introduces herself as Jane Newton. This makes the receptionist apologize after Jane hands out a tip.

I'm sorry, madame, and guys. Please don't let this policy leave the building. It is forbidden to let visitors and the outside world know about this. I don't want to lose my job. I also promise to not tell Him anything, Jazz! I'm a huge fan of yours and have been doing some research on my own. She winks.

Jane is baffled. Is it that easy to find out who Jazz without the suit is? She lets this slide after promising and being promised to keep her mouth shut. There is still one issue. They can't use lifts or escalators because they will need their biometric data, which is what they are trying to prevent. They take a half-hour walk down the stairs to their preferred location, escorted by the receptionist herself.

They walk into the cell and call out Jin's name: *Jin Fangs, are you here?*

Arrghh!! Who the hell is here to bother me again?

He jumps down from his bed and sits in front of Jane. *Well, hello there, beautiful lady...*

Sam is furious but keeps his calm. He asks him if he is really the Jin Fangs they are looking for.

In the flesh, my friends. Your face looks familiar. Are you Sam? And you... You must be Lucius, no, I have seen Lucius before, well, at a younger age, but you don't seem anything like him. You must be the color blue.

It's Blu, B-L-U, not the color blue! Please don't mix up the names! How do you know us? Can you stalk people from within these cell walls?

Jin laughs hysterically. The boys smile due to his contagious laugh.

Alright boys, since you are exactly the ones I'm looking for... Before I tell you anything... Guess my age!

Jane steps closer to him and guesses, *Fifty-six? You look much, much younger, but there must be a reason why you are asking to guess.*

Yes, pretty lady! There sure is a reason. Do you really think I'm that young? How old do I look?

Somewhere between twenty-four and thirty. She answers. Sam makes a joke about him being thousands of years old, and maybe Ions.

*Ding, ding, ding!!!! Korrekt Sam, genau das! You are somewhere near it. Alright.

Sam stops smiling and asks him, *Wait, what? You must be joking... How can you be that old? It shouldn't be! What did you mean, you saw Lucius? You have been here for almost as long as Lucius is alive.*

He ignores to directly answer Sam's question.

Now tell me, Sam, from what you have lived through till now, how impossible does living for this long sound like?

Jane barges into the conversation and says, *True! He also gained his abilities not too long ago.*

So Sam is a late bloomer or a Tomeinei. Your potential must be out of this world!!

Tom what? All three friends ask. They are confused.

So basically, Tomei is the flow of energy. It is the source from which superhuman abilities come. Let's say it gives you control of your inner and astral energy. A Tomeinei is an individual who is awakened by an outer source. This gives him almost an endless amount of capacity to endure. But from my experience, it takes time to use its full potential. A Tomeinei is awakened as soon as his abilities are awakened by an event. Awakening and awakening abilities are two different things. Awakening makes you immortal. The different stages of Tomeinei give you different natural changes. You will have to find out on your own. Awakening abilities, or awakening an ability, means you have gained consciousness of the skill.

Wow! So much information! So I am what is called a Tomeinei. One important question... You knowing what it means, and being this old means that...

Jin smiles at him and answers, *Yes, you could say I am a Tomeinei; it's still not clear what exactly I am; I am a god. Perhaps you know exactly who I am?! You don't need to hide or hold back, Sam!*

Sam whispers to Jane and Blu, trying to find out who Jin truly is, and they find out something interesting.

Jin, why weren't you imprisoned somewhere in Continent F? That's where you came from and lived, isn't it? Jin laughs at his question and counters Sam, *That's all you could come up with? After this long discussion? Ok, do you know the name of this prison? It is your hint!*

Wait... the Monkey King? Nooo, it can't be!

Why not? I'm surprised you haven't even tried seeing through me! Are you not yet able to do so? It's a perk of a Tomeinei, it's one of the first skills that awakens.

Jane explains to Jin about the superhuman-dampener she has found in the blue prints. Sam realizes something. His passive skill, "god's seventh sense," is still active.

Yeah, about that. There is a dampener, and it's just for me. Every other person is safe in here. I wonder how you got in here because it is forbidden for your skin to enter, and it's because of my descendants. That's not important right now. Now try doing it. Concentrate on me and find a spot in me you can track. Then track it all the way down to my core. Start by looking deeply into my eyes, waiting for me to look into yours. It doesn't matter how fast I look away again. As long as you concentrate on it, you should be good. I will help you out if you get lost somewhere in there. So concentrate on my eyes. They will lead you into my gateway. Because I'm dampened, it should be an easy task for you. Though I have to warn, I have a very powerful consciousness. My will might still be too much for you, even in a dampened state.

Sam follows Jin's instructions and looks deeply into his eyes. *Got it!* He whispers. He goes down the rocky path of Jin Fangs. He relives Jin's past and present. He pulls closer to him and holds his skull. Sam's pupils widen as Jin's retract. Sam's abilities are powerful to control. He is able to see every dimension of Jin instead of just one. *Enough, how are you doing this? I didn't expect this. Something like this shouldn't be possible! Stop!* Sam goes much deeper and finds another consciousness in Jin. He wakes him up and talks with him. It is Anansi. Sam forcefully grants him his freedom by looking into his core after scanning him, making him able to partially activate Jin. *Wake up, Jin! We've got work to do!* Anansi shouts at Jin and awakens a larger part of his Tomei.

Jin is back to one-hundredth strength. The dampener still holds him back, but he can use his abilities to an extent. He tries pushing Sam back. Sam falls in deeper. *How are you doing this? Wait, I have met you before. I have sensed your presence before! It's you! Or not? You are darkness—different than the first time we met! Whatever, get out!!!* Sam pulls out and explains everything he has seen. He tells his friends about his new plan to eliminate Jin's friend, Morphius.

Chapter 38

Everyone agrees with Sam's plan.

But how did you come up with something so effective this fast? Jane is astonished.

*What do you mean? I was gone for days! Sorry, Jin, I took my time, sat there, and watched everything peacefully. I had to learn some new abilities too. You have awesome skills! I had to tap into your feelings and find the best solution. You were a great help because you have been making your own plan ever since he visited you.

It's hard to see an old friend you grieved over come back and betray you. Anyways, his being here is a problem for me, and I want him out. I think it's time to start putting myself first, above others, and I'm going to start by getting rid of him. His existence challenges my future, and I can't have that! We've got to call out Lucius and John. There is work to do. As for you, Jin, you will have to wait a little longer. I heard the higher-ups talk about the day you guys will be released, and that's gonna be real' soon! That's why I have planned out everything so that you will be able to join in late. Just in case we can't beat him alone.*

Are we going to ignore the fact that you were gone for a minute and claim it was days? Jin asks.

Sam shrugs his shoulders.

Jane stands in front of Sam and tells everyone that his plan is final.

They walk out and leave Jin and his friends behind. Jin doesn't bother arguing about anything, as he has seen and understood Sam's will. *That dude is no joke!* He thinks.

Blu, of course, doesn't miss the opportunity to train with his cousin and Jane. They train every morning before leaving for studies and every evening, leaving behind any close relatives and friends.

After the first week, Lucius accepts Blu's invitation to train together. John, as well, finds out about their plan and decides to become stronger with them.

Becoming stronger in just a month—that's the dream!

Jane has been doing her best to keep up with the boys. Her suit has been upgraded with new and improved layers. Each outer layer is up to a hundred times stronger than the previous and more powerful when combined. Sam senses more abnormalities in her than before. Her body is adapting to her new life.

Jane, I think you are manifesting some kind of inhumanity. Your energy flow has changed, and it is roaming around freely. It has taken on the color blue. Beautiful, quiet, and free, just like the sky on a bright day. I think we should soon start working on putting it to use. I need to think about the "How."

Lucius has forgiven Sam for being the Jazz he hates. He finds the confidence to ask him about his weakness. *Yo Sam, you see... I can manifest flames, but somehow I keep burning myself when I use them, so I haven't been using them for a while now. Do you think there is something that could be done to make it work?*

Sam is happy to hear Lucius open up to him. He smiles and tells him that *there is an easy fix for this.* It isn't that much of a problem for him to figure it out. While testing out his theories, Sam discovers another ability of his: summoning flames. Though his flames are quite different, each time he summons them without focus, they appear as white, blue flames.

John tells everyone that he has an old friend who might have given him the answer to Lucius' problem(s). Sam asks, *Did your friend, by any chance, say something about his energy flow not being put to use?*

Yes, he even had a name for it. Let me think... Was it something about Tomi? Tomo? Tome? No, what was it again? He tries to recall the name he has forgotten.

Sam fills in and asks, *Tomei?*

Yes! John shouts. *He said it is written differently than spoken. It is written T-o-m-e-i.*

*I never knew how it was written. I thought it was exactly how you pronounce it. Something like, *Tobb-e-a-n. Cool, now I have learned something new. Your friend, though, must be very wise to know something like that. He must be like us and really old.*

John answers without hesitating, *Yes! But I don't quite know what he can do. He always knows what I want and need before I even bother to ask. He might be something like a mind-reader or something. Also, he can create a sphere and freeze anything within it. He says that all his abilities are limited to some extent. Like distance and space-stuff. I don't know, he talks a lot! He tells stories, too. He knows almost everything.*

Lucius has been listening to their conversation and hates being left out. *Hey, hey, what about filling me in and helping me? Stop making it all about yourselves!*

They explain to him that he has to let out his Tomei. Like electricity flowing through a device, he has to make his Tomei flow outside his body to cover his skin. The flames are manifested as his ability to create through magic. Manifesting flames means to ignite them through magic, and the skin is „allergic" to them. He has to willingly make his energy flow circularly and exit exactly where he wants to ignite. He is to imagine himself being lighter. First, he lets his energy flow out like gas and then ignites it to sustain it. The outflow of Tomei is magic. It is the burning gas, as well as oxygen. It holds every element needed for a specific skill, but not every existing element.

Theoretically, every supernatural being can create, for example, flames. Depending on how it is created, one either loses his energy or is able to sustain his flames longer. An elemental magician, here: a fire magician, can easily summon flames without using Tomei. He sustains his flames by pushing through a little amount of Tomei to keep them "alive." The more he summons, the greater the flame.

By summoning a large amount of flame and compressing it, the flame changes color and intensity. It can become blue and burn hot in a beam or on a single strip as a laser. A magician who isn't of the fire element will have to create flames. First, one lets the required amount of Tomei flow out of the body before creating the flames. Here, the speed can vary, depending on how skilled the magician is. The flames created do not hurt the user while he holds them.

The user is naturally coated at the exact spot where the flames appear. Summoning is of outer nature (out of thin air), and creating is of inner nature (Tomei manipulation).The main difference between creating and summoning is that the creator loses his Tomei quicker than the summoner.

This again!? Sam keeps hearing a voice in his head.

You have to train your energy flow in such a way that you use less than you refill in a period. That's how I manage mine, though I have more than enough. Tomei is powerful; it can sustain strong spells or abilities with just a small amount. It's all about practice. Do you think you can do it?

Everyone takes on Sam's advice and works on the inner and outer energy flow.

After a month, they are able to control their Tomei—not as good as Sam wishes, but enough to hold onto their strongest abilities for ten minutes.

Guys, the day has come! I have bought some clothes for you. All you have to do is let your Tomei flow through them so they aren't completely destroyed in battle by your abilities. Everyone, suit up! It's time to go and beat some Morphius-ass!

Okaaayy, let's go! Jane screams. Everyone is surprised.

Yo, somehow you are becoming as weird as Sam! Blu adds.

Everyone laughs.

Chapter 39

Sam and his friends visit Jin for the last time before his release. They tell him to rush to the battlefield "as soon as" he gets out of prison. He agrees and tells them, *Guys, I'm very sorry, but I was stupid enough to not keep my mouth shut. You will know what I'm talking about real soon!* *Again, very sorry!* He repeats.

Sam keeps a serious face.

I think I know what you have done, but that doesn't change the fact that it will all be over soon. Question is, for whom will it be over?

After thirty minutes of conversation, they take off for their new destination: Stonehenge, the place Jane's father has seen him. There, they see a man in a white robe sitting in between the heel stones.

Is it him? Jane is curious. She tells everyone to stand still while she walks slowly to the man who appears to be meditating.

He notices someone coming nearer and lifts up his hands.

Guilty!! He says with a calm voice. *And now what?* He asks with a change of voice, sounding more arrogant than he looks. Jane is surprised by his appearance.

Oh wow, you really don't look old at all. I was looking forward to seeing someone a little older and scarier. Are you really the man called Morphius?

Suddenly, a large, white piece of cloth swirls from below around his body. It covers him and transforms into a robe. He drops his hands.

Bingo!

He snips on both hands and continues, *Well, if you are here, it means you aren't in the mood to talk, just like me! I hoped you prepared yourselves to never go back home!?*

He snips again and twirls his right index finger after lifting his hand. With this motion, he summons a dark cloud to surround him.

You didn't really think I would stand here alone to face you, did you? To fight a king, no, a god like me, you need to prove yourselves worthy. There is no facing me if you can't even make your way up here. Now, say your goodbyes to your beloved world! His voice echoes throughout the cloud.

The cloud grows larger and shoots out red and black lightning. It's core's color changes to white. It unleashes soldiers who walk out elegantly, taking off their hats.

Now it's time to show me who you are! Morphius screams.

Sam stares unimpressed and asks him if it is all he's got.

Like, to be honest, I was hoping you had something extremely dangerous up your sleeves. Now I'm just looking at soldiers and amateur Gene Zs. The question is, do we eliminate them or just make sure they never get to move freely ever again?

Morphius feels insulted by Sam's words. He screams out, *Sam!!* and enlarges the cloud.

Ohhh, it gets bigger and bigger!

This time, Sam gives off a satisfied reaction.

So this is how you do it!

Blu looks at his cousin. He observes his reactions and eye movements towards Morphius' attack.

Sam? Have you figured out something yet?

Yes! I think I have learned a new move. It isn't an ability he is using. He claims.

Lucius is interested in their conversation and wants to know what they are talking about. He asks Sam what he is on about, to which he replies, *This guy is using magic. He is casting a spell to do whatever he is doing, and I like the way he does it. He doesn't cast his spell by screaming out embarrassing words like we do. He is using his hands to make signs. I have studied it enough to know what each movement means.*

There is silence among them. Jane hears everything Sam says through her earpiece and draws back to the boys.

Hey, are you sure about what you are saying?

Yes!! I am going to use this battle to teach you guys. All you have to do is react fast and do exactly what I tell you to do.

John asks how his plan is going to work, not knowing Sam can, with focus, see everything that is happening at once. Blu explains to him this ability.

Alright, Blu, left! John, right! The rest of us will move twenty seconds after you and freestyle. The soldiers are mine. Your goal is Morphius! Blu and John, you guys have to walk normally till the twenty seconds are over! Lucius, clench your fingers and fully raise both index and middle fingers. Push them together and flex your muscles. Notice! Your hands and fingers aren't allowed to touch. After pushing, you have to pull them apart with the exact same restraint. Focus on jumping down from above Morphius and jumping backwards. Be ready to attack! Alright, guys, go! Go! Go!

They move according to Sam's plan. He makes one hundred signs in a second and dashes off. He creates wormholes through which he jumps from one end of a dimension, through the battlefield, to the next dimension. His movements are accelerated through the jumps, and he eliminates the soldiers one after the other. During the fight, he creates new temporal wormholes and explains what signs are needed to create them. Lucius jumps down from the skies after five minutes.

Hey, am I too late, or why are you guys almost done with the soldiers? How long was I gone for? Sorry for missing the party! Wooohooo!!

He summons fire through his fists and creates a huge firefist.

Hell's giant!

Morphius sees his attack and pulls back to counter. *You found out that there are no soldiers left and decided to attack the king. That's the wrong move, kid!!*

He grabs onto thin air and rotates his fist ninety degrees inward. His fist becomes white and cold.

Hot icicle!!

He hits Lucius's „hell's giant" and overpowers him. Lucius is sent back into the skies but manages to think fast and make new signs, followed by the exact same signs over and over again. He makes the same signs seven times and gets thrown from one void to the other. He targets Blu, picks him up, and jumps through more voids with him.

Blu now understands the signs and copies them. They fly from Morphius' left and right, open new voids beneath him, and push him through them. Sam sees their effort and invents new signs that no one has ever seen before. He creates a barrier and infinite voids in between them.

Judgemental space!!!

He screams out the name of his attack and stretches out his left hand towards the void, through which Morphius falls, while the right hand points to the highest point of his attack.

Bang! A loud bang fills the atmosphere, and Morphius strikes down with his arms smashed. There is no sign of life in him.

Chapter 40

Somewhere on a continent now called Continent A.

Once on a continent with the most trustworthy worshipers of Zeus, a woman named Martha prays to Zeus to help her. Her man has left her behind after their engagement, promising her to come back after five years. She loves her so much that she misses him after the first few months and prays through chanting that he will come back sooner than he has promised.

She has rejected every other man who dares to ask for her hand in marriage. After half a year, she yearns for her man and doesn't believe she can live another month without him by her side.

Almighty Zeus! Your servant is calling upon you! I have been waiting for an eternity to see him again—the man of my dreams, the seed of my future fruits, the love of my life. I will never fall in love with anyone again if he doesn't come back to me. I have a weird feeling in my abdomen, and I can't take it anymore. Please help me, your humble servant. Make him come back to me, make him appear earlier than promised, make him fill my heart, and clear this emptiness, I beg of you.

Her prayer reaches Zeus. He sends thunder down to earth to comfort her. He appears as an eagle in her dreams and promises her a happy life. He reappears every night to speak with her and take her mind off the love of her life. He gifts her with perfect sight and more beauty than any woman on earth. He cleanses her from her sorrows and pain. He tells her stories.

Very soon, Zeus finds a liking for her; he falls in love with the most beautiful woman mankind has ever witnessed and becomes selfish toward her. He no longer has the intention to grant her her greatest heart desire and unleashes war on earth.

The first three years have passed, and the world is unsafe. Women are kept at home, and men are sent into war to fight for their families. Any intruder who dares enter Martha's house is punished by Zeus himself; this attracts the attention of the other gods. They are not happy about the situation. They lack the power to stop Zeus and watch the strongest Olympian break their very first rule: "No god shall ever unleash an unstoppable war on humans."

After one and a half years, four and a half years after Martha's man leaves her behind, Zeus offers peace under one condition: Martha will give him a chance and praise him with her body for one night.

Martha, missing her lost man and hoping that he has survived the war so far, agrees to take his offer. Zeus shows her passion and gives her the night of her life. He devours Martha and savors every piece of her to keep the memory. Soon after this, he single-handedly stops the war and creates a new rule: "No god shall ever touch a human or live amongst them until it is of Zeus' order."The gods aren't happy with this decision. Not knowing what Zeus has done, they silently agree on the rule and banish themselves from Mother Earth.

In the first six months after Zeus disappears from her life, Martha isn't aware of her pregnancy. Her belly stays almost flattened, and the baby goes unnoticed. Her period is considered to have stopped because of sickness and heartbreak. She puts herself at fault and punishes herself by eating only plants and drinking less water than usual.

Her man returns after five years have passed and tells her about his experience. He has been cheating on her with multiple other women and is finally ready to settle down and have kids with Martha.

She doesn't care about her man's sins. *He came back to me!* She thinks.They spend their first night together. He gives his all to impregnate his woman and asks for her hand one last time. This time, they will marry. They plan to marry in three months.

A day before their wedding, Martha's belly grows large over night, and an unknown presence kicks in.

You are a witch! The time hasn't yet come to bear fruit. You are an untruthful woman, Martha! He screams at her and barges out of their home. He never returns.

Martha lives, gives birth to a handsome baby boy, and names him Morpheus. The villagers disown her due to her unfaithfulness, not knowing the story behind it all. She moves to Continent C and begins a new life. She raises her demi god of son to become humble and help humans. She gifts her most precious blessing before she dies: a strong heart.

Morpheus travels throughout Continent C, shows believers miracles, and promises their safety. In return, he will guard and heal them. He will play god over them. He does this to not catch Zeus' attention.

One day, he meets two individuals: Jin and Silvester. He travels around the world through time after being saved. In a fight against Poseidon, he loses friends. To them, Morpheus has been killed in a battle.

He survives, and he plans revenge. He wants his old friends to feel what he has felt: pain, anger, hatred... Morphius lives through the most beautiful events in history. He lives through stories, time, electricity, physics, and general science.

The day of his revenge has come. His plan doesn't go as perfectly as he planned, but he gains something better in return. He gains freedom over his body. He is set free from the earth's boundary. Now, his goal is to take manners into his own hands and finish what he has started. He gains control over the forbidden technique.

Chapter 41

Everyone on the battlefield pauses to take in what has happened. With a single attack, Morphius has lost his arms. There is no sign of him breathing, and there is no sign of his heart beating.

Is he dead? Sam asks himself.

He walks into the barrier. He presses into Morphius' neck to check his pulse, and under his nose to check on his breathing.

I thought he had much more to offer... Whatever, let's go!

The barrier collapses, but not of Sam's doing. What is happening? Sam claims that the barrier needs too much energy and time to prepare; therefore, it isn't an option to re-do it in a short time. He needs to learn how to revive a collapsing barrier. He backs out of range and tells everyone to keep their ears covered to protect them.

An unbearable sound pierces through the ground and enters the body. There is no chance of protection against it. They freeze on the spot after the exposure. Lucius and Sam, the closest to the barrier, see a miracle: Morphius' limbs are growing back. Every scar and skin damage is resetting.

His heart beats the deepest bass, and the ground trembles. The air surrounding them visibly swirls around and flows directly through Morphius' nose. His arms spread to the side and slightly drop down while his body ascends and turns over with his face looking into the heavens. His back arches. His legs and arms spread wider apart. The dust and rocks on the battlefield roll underneath him and rise to protect him, surrounding him in a perfect sphere.

Lucius tries walking towards him as soon as his body begins to move but is held back by Sam, who appears to be frightened of what will happen next.

Stand back; I have a very bad feeling!

A massive void appears from above the skies. A giant, glowing creature appears. A godly creature, a king wearing a spikey, flakey crown. Over his crowned skull, there is a golden halo hovering brighter than a flashlight.

Lucius calls out, *I've seen that staff before! It's the Monkey-King!*

Jane looks up and shouts, *Jin!!* with tears running down her face after she deactivates her helmet.

You finally came! I hoped it wouldn't be too late.

He stares down at Sam and shakes his head. He raises his right arm and opens a new void, through which he summons his men. They are officially free.

Alright, I need to make god-mode a little smaller...

He shrinks to his normal size with his "god-mode partly activated and points his staff toward the flying sphere.

Jin isn't impressed, though he claims to be surprised by how the event has turned out.

So this is what it looks like to be reborn as a true god! I have read about it, but there has never been anyone to reach this state. This is the highest awakening to be witnessed to date. You could say he is in the zone. The scripts say that the weakest soul will die within the first few minutes, but Morphius... He isn't weak. As soon as the dirt sphere disappears and he is not dead, he will be a deadly challenge, a real danger!

He continues, *Hey, you guys!*He points to Morphius' soldiers and warns them: *It will be best to fight with us. Right now, he might want a one-man army, so you will all be useless to him. Meaning he will attack you as soon as he is ready. It's something he liked doing in the old days. You don't mean anything to him if you are too weak!*

The sphere quickly vanishes, but there is no one in it. Jin senses a presence from far above and looks at him. *You don't have to do this!* He claims.

Morphius slowly rolls his eyes downward to look down on them. He stretches out his right arm, widens his palm, and rotates it. Four soldiers fall to the ground and release a red-white ball. Sam runs toward the fallen soldiers and grabs two of the balls before Morphius descends.

Sam hides the balls between his hands and retreats.

Meanwhile, Morphius grabs the other two. He dashes through the crowd and touches each soldier with his yellow-glowing hands. He extracts the soul of every soldier by reaching into their deepest consciousness and calls this ability "chaos after dawn." In doing so, the warmth within deplenishes, and the bodies turn ice cold and pale white. He pushes the balls down his throat in a flash. The soldiers fall to the ground while he consumes the last souls.

*So this is what it feels like, huh?! The strongest Gene Z's taste the best!!*Sam sees what Morphius has done. Without understanding what it is about, he swallows both stolen balls.

Damn, what was that?

Jin grabs Sam by his collar and pins him to the ground. He asks, *What have you done? It is the forbidden technique of the soul. Why did you consume those souls?*

What!?! What do you mean, „consumed a soul"? What is going to ha...?? Sam asks.

He falls to the ground with foam flowing out of every one of his holes. His natural tattoos glow, and his eyelids light up.

Jane, take him home! He is of no use to us and will only hold us back! This is his own doing. I'm sorry, but I don't know for sure if he is going to recover. Just, go!! Hurry!!

Jane re-activates her helmet and grabs Sam. She doesn't stop running until she gets Sam home. *What have you done this time, dude? Don't, don't you dare leave me behind!!* She pats his forehead.

Back to the battlefield...

Jin enlarges himself again and summons his sword.

What happened to you, brother? How far do you want to go? Why would you go this far and take so many lives? Don't you remember why we killed your brother, Ares? Why do you want to take someone else's freedom?

Morphius smirks and appears in front of Jin in an instant. He says, *I have already told you what I need to tell you! I wanted my freedom and my freedom to rule, but every descendant of yours turned his back on me like I was this disease. With my vision, there will be peace.

None will try to claim my throne, and I will decide who deserves to live. Every sin will be punished with death, and of course, I will be rich! I will be both a true god to be worshipped and a king who rules! Don't tell me it isn't enough reason to go this far! You did something similar, remember? Killing gods and sealing them in their own realm? I have given it my all. I have put so much sweat and effort into it. I have even made a failsafe, so nothing goes wrong.

I have the greatest plan ever, and I won't let you ruin this for me! I will have to kill you, your friends, and your family. I know you will always stand in my way and stop me. I learned the hard way! Maybe the oracle was wrong and all these insects with Tomei weren't chosen, right? That's what you told Silvester before, right? Or maybe I am part of the big event.

Now I know every descendant of yours! I have to kill you all, and there is a plausible reason for that. Everything I am going to do to you today is show mercy; this is showing my respect to my only best friend to ever exist. I could have hurt you deeply, but I have decided to put you to sleep peacefully. THIS IS ALL BECAUSE YOU ARE MY BEST FRIEND, JIN! IT'S BECAUSE YOU ARE MY BEST FRIEND! My dearest...*

He breathes out deeply, calms down, and walks around, saying, *I always envied my best friend, but I couldn't do anything about it because I was weak. I couldn't betray you as long as you were alive because I loved you, my best friend! Killing your favorite son hurt me, but it also eased my soul because I envied him and wanted you for myself at the same time. I never did anything wrong! There is truly no reason to regret what I did! It was all because I wanted to be like my best friend—so strong, so powerful! From all this respect, all I got was being left behind! You never saw me for who I was, Jin!*

Tears run down Jin's cheeks as he speaks calmly, *You never told us a thing! You could have informed us that there was something eating you up from the inside. You were never replaced, Mor! It's just, you disappeared after we defeated Poseidon. We... I thought you were dead because of how much of a mess it became. You could have made yourself visible to us, you know! But instead, you chose to stay away. YOU made us believe you were dead.*

Have you even tried putting yourself in my shoes, My - Friend? I don't think so! After I was free, I even created a whole new empire—a city that traded goods with you personally—because I wanted you to find me. I just wanted you to put in a bit of effort to see your „best friend" again. I left hints in the goods you got yourself. You were such an optimist; at least you could have had this slight, tiny piece of hope that something could go beautifully. As a god, you should have shown interest and asked questions. Rather, you decided to enjoy your simplest life. My best friend never noticed me spying on him. You deleted my existence from your head, that genius-filled head! You never tried looking for my „dead body." Do you know how much it is to endure knowing that your best friend left without you?!!

Jin interrupts him after a while. *Did you say free? What do you mean by that?*

The nature of Morphius' voice changes. He is sad; his voice shivers, and his pupils twitch. He stops walking in a circle and tells his friend, *There is something I haven't told you. It was supposed to be a secret, but maybe it will help you wear my shoes. I almost died that day, but how would you know, right? The ruler of Atlantis captured me as they were looking for Poseidon's body... They were looking for the body of their beloved FRIEND!

First, they wanted to use me to lure you in, but they gave up because you defeated f*cking Poseidon! They would stand no chance against you. So what did they do? They had no choice but to cure me. It may sound like a positive gesture to treat an injured person. They treated me as slowly as possible because I was to take upon every anger they had against you and pain you made them suffer.

Your sin created a silent war, which one man had to pay for alone! That's where it came to mind. Why not punish sinners? I started with their leaders after my treatment was done. My second awakening accelerated the process. The second awakening is near death; I survived it. My abilities grew stronger, and my magic became phenomenal. Well, what happened afterward, I have already told you. If you still don't get why this is the only way, then I'm sorry, but I can't say goodbye to you.*

He shows his finger-grown claws and stabs Jin with them before he can react. He pulls them out and shoots Jin away. *Air blast!**Now you will get to know how far I am willing to go! You better defend yourself, because I am not holding back!*Lucius and Blu rush in to help Jin. They fight for three hours.

And then...

Morphius creates his strongest attack, one he has never used or trained for before. It is a one-time attack, which exhausts him. It blows away Blu and Lucius, and it pushes Jin to the ground. His crown falls off and leaves a deep scar.

It is supposed to be an unmovable crown...

He stays on the ground and looks his best friend emotionlessly in the eyes. Jin holds Morphius' hand. He knows his best friend isn't going to spare him, now that he has the chance to finish what he has started.

You shouldn't have joined the fight! You might have lived a few more hours! Warning me about today was your greatest mistake!

He looks down on Jin. His tears flow like a waterfall. He wants to give the last part of humanity away; it should die with his friend.

Take my last tears with you. This is my gift to you as a best friend. I wish things were different between us. After you are gone, I am going to be alone because there will never be anyone to replace you. No one is like you, no one will ever be like you, and none will ever be you!

My best friend, I'm sorry. I will take your burden with me. I hope you don't lose yourself. Take care!

Jin opens his arms, closes his eyes, and smiles.

It is time...

Morphius casts a spell and transforms his hand into a blade. He slowly pushes it through Jin's chest.There is a brief moment of silence in which only the sound of skin tearing and blood gushing can be heard.Jin opens his eyes and sees his staff attached to Morphius' chest.

I, I didn't see that one coming! You weren't fighting with us! How did you...

At the exact same time, Jane sees Sam smile.

Back to the battlefield...

He warned me about the newbie. It's you! Who are you?

Johnny! Remember the Richardsons? Yeah, I'm their biological son. The first human to have the Gene Z

I miscalculated! So they did have an offspring... Kid, how does it feel to kill for the first time? Jin's staff has already started altering your mind. You are too weak to wield it. Now that you have my blood on your hands, what are you going to do? Are you ready for the consequences? What are you going to do, now that you have singlehandedly taken revenge on your parents's deaths?

... John sobs.

One more disappointment before I go: you aren't the first Gene Z user; my son is! Because of him, I found out that normal human beings can inherit superpowers. He has used the formula on his daughter, whom I will duell with after I die. I made sure she was my failsafe. She will grow stronger with me inside her, as creepy as it sounds. My death is the beginning of our deal. How do you think you are going to stop that? Of course, John will be her first target. It's exactly like I said—my blood is on your hands! Hahahahahahaha! Morphius laughs silently.

With his voice slowly fading away, he asks Jin, *Hey Jin?*

Morphius?

The guy who was taken away—who was he?

You mean Sam?

Huh! So it was him!

That dude is dangerous; you have to end him as soon as you get the opportunity to.*Why should I?*

He is the cursed one. It feels like I have met him before. Back then, he was filled with light, but today, he is full of darkness! I am very sure that he is the only one I have been afraid of. He is older than he looks.

Hmm I will find out myself. I will keep an eye on him, promised!

**You better do it or else... You will be doomed! You shouldn't trust him! And that girl—I think she will betray each and every single one of you guys if he wants to. I have never felt such a bond between two individuals before. Call me crazy, but today I was able to see what love is. I'm glad I did before dying. You might want to end him before you can get to her. It seems like this is the last gift you will ever get from me. Take care, best-friend!*

He coughs and spits blood before his body fades away.

Chapter 42

Nine months later, 2042.

Jane and Blu wonder why Sam hasn't woken up yet. The world has been a mess ever since the puppet master was eliminated. His men in authority have all quit; they know what might happen if they continue with his dynasty. Jin has spoken to them and warned them about the consequences. He visits Sam for the first time, hoping to find a solution to his unconsciousness.

So you have finally decided to show up, huh? You do know that it's disrespectful to leave a man behind—the man whose idea it was to get rid of a serious problem of yours, right?

Yeah, yeah, I know. I'm sorry, but I had to take care of important things. What matters is that I am here now and might be able to help him out. So, you are saying he hasn't opened his eyes, not even once, ever since... You know?

Mhmm, sure! Let me guess, you had to make the world a better place?

Yeah, something like that... Jin says with confidence.

Blu steps in between them and holds them apart. *You guys need to stop! It's about Sam now, this would be his chapter if our lives were to be a written story. So please, just... What can you do about him, Jin?*

Jin is clueless. He came by without a plan. The first thing that comes to mind is the most complex thing he can do.

Maybe I can tap into his consciousness like he did mine?!

Jane disapproves of Jin's suggestion. She asks him, *Should this be some kind of revenge to prove that you can also go deep into his head like he did yours? I don't want you to! Besides, it is going to hurt you. He isn't that easy to read or tap into, you know? He is going to kick your ass in there. He will put you to sleep and give you a goodnight kiss on your forehead.*

Blu laughs at Jane's comment, *Are you for real now? Ok, now I am sure you are becoming like him, ahahahaaa! Hey Jane, I know you aren't happy about what Jin did, but he might really be the only one to help us out. Maybe you are right, and Sam isn't going to let him in that easily... Maybe someone whom Sam trusts should go with him.*

Sam trusts no one! He has said it multiple times, and I know he means it. Maybe someone really close to him? He has been talking about a sister he has never met. We could go find her.

He says that because his sister died right after birth. I know. He keeps talking about him having the feeling that she is alive somewhere, but it's just his anxiety or and his craziness. He's crazy sometimes. He doesn't have a sister. Someone close could work, and I know exactly who!

Who is it? And by the way, it's and/or! Jane asks curiously.

Really? Did you mean to ask that question? Today is an important day for this person.

His mom?

Come on! It's the twenty-seventh of September; come on, man! It's me! Today is my birthday, guys! I am the one. After all, I am his favorite cousin. Well, at least that's what I call myself.

Oh really? I'm sorry, Blu! I didn't know. Alright then, do it!

Jin? What are you doing? They see Jin kissing Sam on the lips. He believes that it might have something to do with a fairy tale, "The Sleeping Beauty." He asks both Blu and Jane to help out.

Well, at least we tried. This is my first time kissing him, and he isn't even awake to feel it. Jane runs her right index finger over her lips as she speaks. Deep down, she wants to take Sam's place. She would rather suffer than see him suffer. She squishes Blu's cheeks and tells him to give his best and bring him back. She needs to tell him about the ownership she has been keeping from him for a while.

The boys sit on opposite sides, with Sam in between them. They place their hands on his chest and concentrate on getting to him.

Come on, dude, wake up.

An invisible wave pushes them apart. Jin stays on the ground and rethinks his idea. *So, you were right. He didn't let us in. He is like a ticking time bomb. The more we push to do the unwanted, the more we are going to make the situation worse! Do we have any better ideas?*

Blu snobs and suggests that Jane go inside with Jin. He explains, *Right now, I think Jane is our only option. He might let her in.*

And why would you assume he would let me in? Not even YOU were let in, and both of you are gifted with this Tomei thing. What can someone like me possibly do? If something happens, I might not survive.

Blu plays the big brother. He steps in front of her and holds her triceps tightly. He rubs on them to comfort her and asks her to look him in the eyes.

What do you see? I'm madly serious here! Trust me, if he doesn't let you in, there is nothing else we can do. You ARE our only option! Please? I will focus and help you out if something goes wrong because you can't enter with your suit.

Alright, ok, I get it, so stop staring at me with those eyes. I think we are both becoming like him; he also gives off that look. She blushes.

Ohh, is someone interested in him?

It's not like that! And even if I were, I don't think he wants anything from me. I usually push the boys away from me. I'm surprised he hangs out with me. I don't deserve him. I also don't want to ruin our friendship. What if I ask him out and he says no? ...Back to the main topic: what do I do now?

Jin laughs and claims that first she needs to understand how love works.

You just hold my hand and place the other on any part of his body.

Jane places her left hand on his cheek while the other holds Jin's. She closes her eyes and only focuses on Sam; she locks out everything around her.

Sam, where are you?

She enters a raw realm.

Raw realm: This is an unfinished reality. It can be compared with a universe a moment after the big bang. There are no rules yet. A consciousness creates its realm after awakening. A Tomeinei creates a „big bang" after awakening. Depending on how powerful this individual is, the realm can be infinitely large. A known reality is only created after the user or ruler becomes conscious of its existence. Only then can he create rules and control the realm. Sam's realm is covered with darkness, a pinch of white glowing and fading with the darkness, with red lightning bolts in one's location. Further away, all is dark.

Where is Jin? she asks herself.

Jin never entered in the first place. She is alone in an infinte world.

At a further distance, she sees a man hovering in the nothingness with a low white glow around him.

Sam?

She runs closer. It is Sam. He is lying and resting with his eyes wide open. He turns over to her and asks her what is happening to him. He has given up on finding his way home. He is lost and has been roaming around for almost a thousand years.

Or so it feels...

Are you real?

Yes! And I need you to come back home with me!

How can you still be alive after all these years?

What do you mean all these years?

I saw how long you have been sitting right next to me the entire time. You have been visiting me every day for years. At some point, I lost track and ended up here. I don't know what all this is. I feel powerful and weak at the same time. I see everything, but somehow I see nothing. My hearing is all over the multiverse, but I can hear anyone. I don't know which one of these is real and which one isn't. Jane, I'm full of energy, but deep inside, I don't know how much is left. Something is wrong; I don't feel anything at all! Someone has been trying to get to me for the past few years. I only opened up because I saw you. Even right now, he is still trying. So I am going to ask you again... Are you real? And how can you be alive for so long?

Jane knows that he is serious and doesn't prolong the conversation. She promises him that she is real and explains what has happened as well as what is happening. She comforts him by sitting by his side and helping him sort out all of his senses. After another five hundred years in the realm, Sam learns to create a habitable realm; this helps them on their way out.

Buzzing sounds...

Sam wakes up just to see Blu and Jin watching him patiently.

You good?

They nod. Jin slaps his thighs and tells them that his work is done.

There is nothing left to do for you. You seem totally healthy, and you haven't lost your mind. My men and I are going to explore the world. They witnessed the fight against Morphius and have decided to join me as my disciples. If you mess up, I will be here to sort things out and punish you. Don't mess things up! Oh, and take good care of Jane!!

He walks out of the apartment and shuts the door behind him. He misses his timing to lean on, falls back, and leans on the door to breathe out heavily.

What the hell is that? What happened to him? All I felt was suppressing darkness! This man is a true danger!!

Epilogue

After Jin leaves the room...

Sam turns to Blu and says, *Happy birthday, my favorite cousin!*

He hasn't forgotten about his cousin; Jane has told him what day it is. He gives Blu a breathtaking hug, literally! Jane asks if it is a joke about Blu's birthday.

No, it really is! Today, he is fourteen years old.

He never told me about his birthday. Ok, I never asked him. So your birthday is the twenty-seventh of September? Happy birthday, Blu! You are an amazing dude; keep it up!

They walk downtown to the shopping street to get Blu a gift. Sam places his arm around his neck and asks why he isn't with his family.*But you are my family! I would rather hang out with you guys. I'm happy, plus, I think you will get me the most awesome gift ever! AWESOME AWESOMe AWESOme AWESome AWEsome AWesome Awesome awesome some some ssss.* He echoes into both Sam's and Jane's ears.

You don't need to do that! Alright, I guess now we are supposed to get you something awesome, isn't it?

Blu finds himself the most beautiful earphones and a jacket. He leaves Sam and Jane to pay.

*Thank you, guys! Now I'm good to go till my fifteenth!

I've got something to tell you guys! Sam is serious. The friends wonder what he needs to talk about to make such a serious face.

Jane looks him twice in the face and guesses what he wants.

You mean the gadget to travel around, don't you? It's all done, so I'm ready if you guys are...

No, just me!

Jane isn't happy about Sam's decision. She argues with him about not wanting to stay behind after all the work she has put in. Blu insists on joining them, but Sam declines his request.

Ok, Jane comes with me, and Blu stays behind! We have to take a semester break and do what we have to do. I know we are in our final semesters, but there is no other way, and it isn't a good idea to wait for too long. Blu, I can't take you with me!

What do you mean? I can just go with you guys and repeat the classes I will miss. I am pretty smart, and you know that! So just ta...

NO!! You have to stay! Focus on school and your abilities. I promise that next time you will come with us, k? I don't know what awaits us, and we aren't sure if the device will work as planned. Until then, we have to do this alone. Just trust me on this one!

Blu trusts his cousin more than any other person he knows. He agrees to stay behind and let his favorite people do what they have to do.

Promise me that next time you will not leave me behind! I need to hear you say it...

Alright, Blu, I promise to you that next time, you will be on the top list of our traveling adventure, as long as you hold your part of the deal, which is: You will give your best at school and train to become powerful. You will join forces with Lucius and John and be so powerful that not even I will recognize you guys, deal?!

Deal!! I will give my all to surpass you; you just wait!!

Sam and Jane smile after accepting his dedication.

On their way back to Sam's apartment, Jane finds the courage to tell him about a secret she has been keeping for a while.

My parents are about to kick me out of the house, Sam! He is confused. Why should a parent do something this cold-hearted? He asks her where she is supposed to live and offers to let her live with him in his apartment.

Jane looks to the side and tells him, *yeah, about that. I was gonna ask you to help me and live in our house...*

His face explains his confusion, now more than ever.

Our house? Wait, I don't even have enough to manage and buy my own house. Even splitting the cost of a house will be a challenge for me. What are you talking about? Oh, you are joking, right?

Jane is nervous. She wants to find a way to explain her situation without Sam thinking weirdly about her.

So, I got a very undeniable deal cuz the owner of a building wanted to get rid of it. He claims he is an old man who has no kids. I once met him at Anicon. He is very funny, like really funny and stuff, and he is nice. He told me he has no one to inherit it and doesn't know what to do with all he's got. He also gave me a fair price for other things and buildings he has, but I told him I would get to them later. Well, so I bought the first building, and it is really huge. I thought maybe putting both our names on it wouldn't be that bad of an idea.

Sam asks her why she has chosen him to be one of the owners and not her mom or dad. She explains that it is because he "might or might not be" her favorite person.

It also isn't a bad idea because living in an owned home means you don't have to pay rent and stuff, you know?

Ight, I get it! Even though it would have been better to tell me or ask me first, It doesn't matter. So what's the catch about this building? Where is it, how large is it, and what has to be repaired or reconstructed all around it?

Let's get there first; it's not that far away from here. Should we consider buying the rest of his belongings? Fair and cheap price, and he wants to be put to sleep soon. He was talking about this new invention where the body is frozen to sleep to be released in the late future. Maybe he wants to put everything he has into an investment to make it more worth it when he comes back to life.

On their way to the building, they encounter a young man in the cleanest clothes they have ever seen, all white: shirt, pants, jacket, shoes, socks, hat... Even his striped gray hair looks more white than gray, and there is not a single sign of dirt particles on him. He looks at Jane with the most handsome, widest smile one can ever imagine. Sam whispers in Blu's ear, *That man looks clean as f*ck, like an angel or something. Also, there is something pure inside of him. Is this what a pure soul looks like?*

Hey, Jane! How have you been doing? Have you made up your mind yet? Did you talk to him about it? I...

Yes, I just told him about it, and we are on our way to the first one. Would you mind explaining it further to him? She answers.

Blu and Sam immediately understand what is going on. He smiles at Sam, and Sam smiles back. He thanks Sam for his kind words.

Yes, I did hear what you boys were talking about. I am special somehow.

The three men understand themselves as if they have been friends their entire lives. He introduces himself officially. His name is Isaac.

Pleasure meeting you, Isaac. I'm Sam, and this is my cousin Blu.

Ohh, the pure-hearted general Blu? he asks.

Isaac tells Sam everything he has wanted to tell Jane. His deal is hard to deny. He cuts down on the price after finding out how much money both of them have. Without thinking further into it, they agree to take it all. They will invest with all they have and make more money out of it. Isaac has buildings and artifacts all around the world. With Jane's wealth and a few from Sam, they invest two point three million in their future.

Maybe Blu can live with us. The large one in Italy will be where we all meet and find solutions to our problems. The three-story buildings can be rented. Jane shares her plan.

They thank Isaac and ask him why he would want to give it all out for such a cheap price. Without saying a word about his reasons, he says goodbye and disappears.The three friends pretend nothing has ever happened on this day and look around at their new home. They discover a lot of renovating to do and plan it all out in just three hours. Sam holds their hands and travels with them to his apartment.

Jane retrieves a wooden box from underneath Sam's wardrope and picks out a device while Blus sits back to tell them that he is going to be staying at Sam's till they get back.

Someone has to make sure it is all clean. I still don't get why you have to go right now; you haven't even prepared yet. It feels like a quick ending to a written chapter!

What do you mean? Sam asks.

I haven't even prepared to cry or realize what it means to leave you go, for God knows how long! A good story's chapter makes this loooong goodbye where both the traveler and the one left behind cry and hug themselves and stuff, you know?

Sam gives him a long, tight hug and tells him, *It's gonna be alright! Besides, it isn't going to be for so long. Technically, it should be like we never left, well, for you. For us, it is going to be a really long time.*

So then, you are going to travel through time and space? You don't have anything to do with time, remember? Just go; I'll be waiting!

He wraps his left arm tightly around Jane's waist and follows her instructions. He is to travel through space, but with the coordinates and settings from the machine.

All you have to do is imagine sending you, me, and the machine somewhere. Let your energy flow through and fill the work of art. Let's see how it works. Fill it all uuuuuuuupp!!

A flash spreads from the device up to the ceiling. They disappear in an instant. Blu looks around after a few seconds.

*I guess he was wrong. Ok, let's just live until they are back!

At Lucius'...

Alright, John, now you can see how much I have evolved. Call me Lucifer, the King of Hell. It fits my name perfectly!